JOURNEY TO THE CENTER OF THE EARTH 3D™

CHOOSE YOUR OWN JOURNEY

THE SEARCH FOR EARTH'S SURFACE

D1468598

Adapted by Justine and Ron Fontes

Based on the screenplay by Michael Weiss and
Jennifer Flackett & Mark Levin

PSS!
PRICE STERN SLOAN

PRICE STERN SLOAN
Published by the Penguin Group
Penguin Group (USA) Inc., 375 Hudson Street, New York, New York 10014, USA
Penguin Group (Canada), 90 Eglinton Avenue East, Suite 700,
Toronto, Ontario M4P 2Y3, Canada
(a division of Pearson Penguin Canada Inc.)
Penguin Books Ltd., 80 Strand, London WC2R 0RL, England
Penguin Group Ireland, 25 St. Stephen's Green, Dublin 2, Ireland
(a division of Penguin Books Ltd.)
Penguin Group (Australia), 250 Camberwell Road, Camberwell, Victoria 3124, Australia
(a division of Pearson Australia Group Pty. Ltd.)
Penguin Books India Pvt. Ltd., 11 Community Centre,
Panchsheel Park, New Delhi—110 017, India
Penguin Group (NZ), 67 Apollo Drive, Rosedale, North Shore 0632, New Zealand
(a division of Pearson New Zealand Ltd.)
Penguin Books (South Africa) (Pty.) Ltd., 24 Sturdee Avenue,
Rosebank, Johannesburg 2196, South Africa

Penguin Books Ltd., Registered Offices:
80 Strand, London WC2R 0RL, England

Library of Congress Cataloging-in-Publication Data is available.

ISBN 978-0-8431-3305-9   10 9 8 7 6 5 4 3 2 1

A MISERABLE MORNING

Max Anderson's breath came in ragged, desperate gasps. His handsome features were tense with deep, animal panic as he ran for his life.

Max glanced over his shoulder, hoping to catch sight of the big beast chasing him through the thick jungle. But his gaze could not pierce the tangle of leaves. Which would be worse: seeing the dreadful beast—or only hearing its heavy footsteps crashing ever closer and closer?

Suddenly, Max stumbled. Before he could catch himself, he fell over a steep stone cliff! He screamed, "Trevor . . . help me!" But no helping hand stopped his fall. As the cliff flashed past, Max's eyes widened with primitive fear. Max screamed again, "Trevor!"

And then Trevor Anderson woke up. He threw the sweaty sheets off his rumpled bed and ran his shaky fingers through his hair. Trevor's brother, Max, wasn't falling. He did not need Trevor's help. Max had been dead for ten years.

Trevor took a deep breath and looked around his messy bedroom. Daylight shone through a crack in the cheap, roll-up shade. Trevor's eyes flickered over to the clock on his nightstand, which read 9:17 A.M. He was late for work again!

Trevor tried to squeeze one last squirt out of a used-up tube of toothpaste, but there just wasn't anything left. Trevor tossed the flat tube in the trash can, looked at it, and thought, *I know how you feel.*

The face that looked back at him from the bathroom mirror used to be handsome. But his frequent nightmares gave the thirty-five-year-old professor a drained expression.

Trevor spat out the faintly minty water into the sink. It was dirty! Not just a-few-specks-of-pipe-rust dirty, but really filthy. Trevor sighed. Plumbing trouble again. Well, he had no time for a shower anyway.

The closet held a selection of empty hangers and dirty clothes piled on the floor. Trevor found one shirt that didn't smell too bad and pulled it over his head without even bothering with the buttons.

As soon as he opened his car door, Trevor remembered the stack of his students' graded term papers that he'd left in his apartment. He ran back for the papers, but when he got back, his car wouldn't start.

Trevor wanted to give up and go back to bed, but Andersons aren't quitters. So he got his bicycle—and forgot the term papers again. Trevor ran back to his apartment, resigned to the fact that it was just going to be one of those days.

After pedaling all the way to the university, Trevor had to face a half-empty auditorium full of bored students. Why didn't they love plate tectonics the way Trevor did? How could anyone not be fascinated by the story of Earth, written in rocks and fossils and carved by glaciers?

Trevor handed back the term papers and tried yet one more time to get the students excited about his favorite subject. He decided to start at the very beginning and with a cartoon. "Once upon a time, 250 million years ago, all the land masses on Earth were one vast super-continent called Pangaea . . ."

On the screen at the front of the auditorium flashed the image of the world when it was new—or as near as modern science can imagine it. "In 1912, Alfred Wegener noticed that South America fits into the curve of Africa, like the pieces of a puzzle. See?"

Trevor heard the loud smack of gum being chewed with too much energy. A girl raised her hand. After another quick smack, she asked, "Is Wegener going to be on the test?"

Trevor sighed. "Wegener is the father of Continental Drift Theory. Yes, he will be on the test." Trevor looked into the chewing girl's eyes. He'd seen more of a spark in the eyes of some cows. Trevor asked, "Why take Tectonics 101 if you're not the least bit interested in it?"

The girl shrugged. "I've got a science requirement."

The rest of the class burst out laughing. Trevor's heart sank. They just didn't care about plate tectonics. The world under their feet flowed in constant, fascinating motion, yet all this meant nothing more to most of his students than a few credits.

Finally the bell rang, and Trevor made his way to the Maxwell Anderson Center for the Study of Plate Tectonics. The sign was the best part of the small facility, which consisted of several obsolete computers monitored by a lonely young lab assistant named Leonard. When Trevor entered, Leonard looked up from his screen and rolled his squeaking stool over to whisper, "Dude, you're not going to be happy."

Trevor glanced through the window of the tiny glassed-in office. His jaw tensed as he recognized the hotshot geochemistry professor, Alan Kitzens. Trevor could think of no good reason for his rival to be in the lab. "What does Kitzens want?" he asked.

Leonard shrugged. "I don't know. But he brought a tape measure."

This day just keeps getting better and better! Trevor thought sarcastically.

Kitzens jumped up to shake Trevor's hand the moment he stepped through the door. "There's my favorite colleague. How's that continental drift class going? Does it get echoey in there with so few kids?"

Trevor winced. Why did Kitzens insist on comparing class size like athletes keeping score? No one cared about learning or science anymore. The university revolved around attendance, finances, and status. "I prefer the smaller classes," Trevor said. "They allow for a more intimate exchange of ideas."

Kitzens smirked. "Oh, one day I'm sure geochemistry will lose its appeal, and I'll say the same."

Trevor looked up from the papers cluttering his desk. "What do you want, Kitzens? It's kind of busy around here."

Kitzens looked over his shoulder at Leonard lazily licking a pudding pop. "Right, well, I'll make it quick then," Kitzens replied. "The university is pulling the plug on your brother's lab." Kitzens smiled, savoring his triumph. "We're folding it into my new Geochemistry Institute expansion. It's going to give us the storage space we need."

Trevor blinked. How could they turn Max's lab into Kitzens's closet?! He stammered, "Isn't the, um, dean supposed to give me this kind of information?"

Kitzens's smile widened. He paused dramatically. "That's the other thing I'm here to tell you."

"No. You?" Trevor's world shook no less than if there had been an actual earthquake.

"Dean Kitzens," the professor purred. "The trustees announce it Thursday." He looked around the lab, noting the placement of the windows and electrical outlets.

Trevor shuddered. What could he do?

Kitzens grinned. "Now you know, my friend, if this was a dean's-office-only decision, I'd let you do your little experiments forever and a day. But science, it's kind of a business and . . ."

Trevor's spine straightened. "First of all, there are no 'little experiments' going on here. This is a place dedicated to Max's big ideas. His original theories predicting volcanic fissures in the mantle—"

Kitzens interrupted, "—have never been proven. How many of your late brother's sensors are even still working out there? One? Two? Across the whole globe?"

Trevor glanced at a computer screen, where three blips blinked in Bolivia, Mongolia, and Hawaii. "Three."

"Once upon a time it was twenty-nine," Kitzens recalled.

"You can't pull the plug!" Trevor interjected. "There's seismic activity in Bolivia and a thirteen-millimeter shift in Mongolia. You do understand that plate tectonics is the key to everything, right? Weather, atmosphere, global warming, predicting the next earthquake, tsunami, or Ice Age!"

Kitzens sighed with boredom. Trevor made the same points at every faculty meeting. "It's been ten years since Max, Trevor. You've done a great job of keeping your brother's work alive, but some projects just run their course. I'm sorry, buddy."

"I'm sorry, too," Trevor said as Kitzens closed the door.

Leonard looked at Trevor's face, threw out the pudding pop stick, and wiped his sticky fingers on his jeans. He logged onto a job search website and scrolled to the "lab assistant" listings. Had he not been so busy looking for a new job, Leonard would have seen the new blip blink to life on a nearby computer screen. The blip flashed near the top of the map, between Greenland and England, on the bumpy little island of Iceland.

Later, after a short bike ride home, Trevor watched the blink-blink-blink of messages on his home answering machine. He hastily emptied his pockets of change, adding to the heap of coins in the large glass jar sitting beside three others also stuffed to their brims with slowly accumulated treasure.

Trevor pushed the button to hear the first message. His sister-in-law's nervous voice asked, "Trevor, are you there? It's Elizabeth. Please pick up. Okay, well, we're on I-95 heading your way."

Trevor's eyes darted to the calendar. Right there in his own handwriting, in bright, red marker in the square for June 28th was the note: SEAN. How could he forget?

Elizabeth's voice went on. "You wanna say hi to Uncle Trevor, Sean?"

Trevor heard the faint negative murmur of his thirteen-year-old nephew.

"He's, um, not in a talkative mood," Elizabeth concluded.

Trevor's stomach sank deeper and deeper as he listened to the second, third, and fourth messages, which tracked Elizabeth and Sean's progress toward Trevor's apartment—and his sister-in-law's growing concern that he might have forgotten about Sean's visit.

Trevor looked around his messy apartment. According to the last message, they were only moments away. Could he possibly get the place presentable in time?

Trevor started to pick some of the empty food containers off the floor. Then the phone rang, and he dropped them all. But instead of answering, Trevor listened as Elizabeth left a final message. "We're pulling up in front of your building. Please don't let me down."

Trevor walked to the window and saw Elizabeth's car pulling up. When she stepped out and looked up, Trevor did not wave. He ducked away from the window, wondering if he could somehow just avoid the whole situation. But it was too late.

Trevor picked up the food containers again, and almost had them in the trash when the doorbell rang—and he dropped them all over again. For a moment, Trevor actually considered pretending not to be home. Then he heard Elizabeth's voice. "Trevor, you in there?"

He sighed, then opened the door to greet the woman Max had loved enough to marry. Trevor remembered dancing at their wedding. Who could have guessed that day would lead to this one? He stammered awkwardly, "I . . . just got in and got your, uh, messages."

Elizabeth frowned. "You forgot, didn't you?"

"What? Of course I didn't," Trevor fibbed. "You think I'd forget?"

Elizabeth looked around the apartment strewn with empty food cartons, dirty socks, and stacks of books and newspapers. She studied Trevor's tired face with serious concern. "You didn't forget?"

"Okay, I forgot it was today," Trevor admitted. "But that doesn't mean I'm not looking forward to the visit, getting some time with the nephew I haven't seen since he was eleven."

Elizabeth corrected him. "Nine," she said.

Trevor blushed. "Wow, nine, right." Then he walked back to the window and looked down at the teenager slumped in the passenger seat of Elizabeth's car. Trevor remembered the day Sean was born, and now the kid was thirteen. Thirteen! Trevor couldn't believe it. "Um, how long is he staying again?"

"Ten days," Elizabeth replied.

Trevor's stomach tightened. "Ten? Yeah? Is that what we said?"

"You said, 'a week to ten days,'" Elizabeth answered.

"Did I, now?" Trevor said as he put on a big smile and walked down to the car to greet his nephew. Sean barely looked up from his hand-held video game.

"Stand up and say hi to your uncle," Elizabeth commanded.

"Hi to your uncle," Sean said.

Trevor searched the teenager's face for the nine-year-old he remembered. "The last time I saw you, you were only this high."

Sean rolled his eyes in disgust. "I've never heard that one before."

Sean dragged his duffel bag out of the car and started to carry it toward the apartment building.

"Hey, mister. Where's my hug?" Elizabeth asked.

Sean put down the duffel and hugged his mother.

"I love you," she said. "Now, you have all my numbers. Your ticket and passport are in your bag. I'll pick you up at the airport in Ottawa. By then I'll have found a house and we can start on our big, new adventure. Pretty exciting stuff, huh?"

Sean turned to his uncle and said, "We get to be Canadians. Thrilling, eh?"

While Sean carried his duffel bag up to Trevor's apartment, Elizabeth spoke to her brother-in-law. "It'll be good for him, being with you." Then she looked into Trevor's eyes and added, "Who knows? Maybe it'll be good for you, too."

Elizabeth opened her trunk and pulled out a cardboard box. "Here. This is for you."

Trevor asked, "More of Sean's stuff?"

"No, it's Max's," Elizabeth said. After ten years, her voice still choked a little on his name.

Trevor was surprised. Death and moving have a way of reminding people of how much stuff they have. Distributing Max's things had been part of the grief Trevor shared with Elizabeth. Ten years later, it seemed, they still hadn't quite finished. Elizabeth said, "Please, just take it."

Trevor nodded and gently took the box from her hands.

When Elizabeth was on her way, Trevor showed Sean his apartment. But since it was only a one-bedroom, the tour didn't last long.

"Wow, nice coin collection," Sean remarked when he saw the four big jars.

"Thanks, it's kind of a pet project," Trevor said.

Then he opened the cardboard box, which was mostly full of old books, but also contained a green butterfly yo-yo and a faded photo of Trevor and Max in their twenties on a mountaintop.

Trevor slipped the yo-yo string onto one finger. "This was your father's version of a video game."

Sean was skeptical. "A yo-yo?"

"Hey, don't laugh. This is physics at work right here. Potential energy, centrifugal force, gravitational pull . . ." Trevor said, trying to remember how to get the tricky toy to do some tricks.

"In ancient times, the yo-yo was used for hunting. Your dad was a magician with this thing."

Sean reached for the yo-yo. "Hey, lemme try that."

Trevor smiled. He wanted Sean to know how special Max was. "Your dad was a man of science. But he could also talk baseball like a scout for the Sox or tie a Spinnerbait in under ten seconds."

Trevor pulled a scrapbook out of the box. He chuckled at a clipping from his childhood with Max. The headline read, ANDERSON BROTHERS WIN SCIENCE FAIR, START THREE-ALARM FIRE. Trevor recalled, "Your grandma used to say we were two halves of the same whole, partners in crime."

Trevor looked into the box again. His lips curled in a nostalgic smile at the sight of a certain well-worn paperback. "Wow," he said. "This was your old man's favorite book: *Journey to the Center of the Earth.*"

Sean glanced at the book. "I think that was on my summer reading list last year. Never got to it."

Trevor tenderly turned to the first page. "Max read it to me when I was a kid."

The yo-yo had captured Sean's attention. While he slung it around on its string, Trevor flipped through the book. He said, "To Max, this wasn't science fiction, it was inspiration."

Trevor noticed numbers in the margins, temperature readings and locations recorded in Max's neat handwriting. "Magma temperatures reach 1,150 in Bolivia, 718 in Mongolia, 753 in . . ."

Excitement rippled up Trevor's spine as he made a startling realization, tingling in anticipation of the moment every scientist craves.

While Trevor was frozen in his "eureka" moment, the green yo-yo crashed into a huge model of a complicated crystal. Dozens of little rods clattered to the floor and small balls rolled everywhere. Sean looked up at his uncle, expecting trouble. Instead, Trevor merely glanced at the mess and asked, "You want to see my science lab, Sean?"

Trevor didn't wait for an answer. He just hurried Sean off to the lab with him. As they entered the building, Trevor muttered, "Something about the numbers in Max's book looks familiar . . ."

He flipped on switches. Fluorescent lights hummed to life. Sean took the yo-yo out of his pocket and did the "walk the dog" trick, making the yo-yo roll across the worn linoleum. The yo-yo returned to Sean's hand like a good green plastic pet.

Sean didn't understand why they had to spend his first night away at some dingy old lab. He just knew they'd miss his favorite TV shows. He asked, "Why can't it wait till tomorrow?"

Trevor rolled across the floor, switching on the computers and babbling with excitement. "Because conditions change. You know what your dad used to say? 'Tectonophysics isn't the science of tomorrow. It's the science of now. It's about seismic events that occur in an instant, once a generation . . .'"

Trevor's eyes flicked over to the screen that now displayed numbers gathered by the remaining sensors from Max's observation network. He stared and swallowed hard before he continued. ". . . once, um . . . or possibly twice?"

Trevor continued to stare at the numbers. "Look at this. Just what I thought: Bolivia, Mongolia, Hawaii—the conditions today are almost exactly like they were in July '97. My God."

Sean studied his uncle's face. The date didn't immediately register. "What's the big deal about July 1997?"

Trevor held Max's old copy of the book up to the screen. He compared Max's margin notes to the glowing numbers. They matched. Then he said, "That was the month your dad disappeared. If this was a 753 instead of a 752, this whole row of numbers would . . ."

As they watched, the 752 changed to 753. The hairs on the back of Trevor's arm tingled as he concluded, ". . . they'd be exactly the same."

Sean's attention had already shifted to one of the other computer screens, the one showing a map of the world and the placement of the remaining sensors. Sean asked, "What do these little blips mean?"

Trevor shooed Sean away from the keyboard. "Hey, don't touch anything. Those little blips are my life's work."

"Four little blips are your life's work?" Sean asked.

Trevor corrected him. "Actually, three little blips."

"I count four," Sean said.

Trevor rolled his chair over to join Sean at the other computer. Sure enough, a fourth blip pulsed near the top of the map, on that bumpy island where Jules Verne's amazing *Journey to the Center of the Earth* took place. Trevor now knew where he had to go, and quickly: Iceland!

They raced back to Trevor's apartment. Sean struggled to understand his uncle's rapid babble. "Things suddenly make sense. When Max saw the readings ten years ago, he took off to investigate, but I never knew where. If the same conditions are repeating themselves, this could be my only chance to find out what happened. Where's your passport?"

Sean asked, "What do you need it for?"

"I'm getting you to Canada a little earlier than we planned." Trevor tossed Sean the worn paperback. "*Journey to the Center of the Earth*. It's all set in Iceland."

Sean flipped through the dog-eared pages filled with neat notes and numbers. His heart fluttered with a sense of closeness to his lost father. "This is all *his* writing?"

Trevor nodded. "Max and I were talking about the possibility of long volcanic tubes stretching into the mantle . . ." Trevor began. "I think that's what Max went looking for, Sean."

The thirteen-year-old blinked. Could his father still be alive somewhere? Or would they at least finally know what had happened to him?

Trevor picked up the phone. "I'm booking you a morning flight to Ottawa, and one for me to Reykjavík." He started dialing.

If you think Sean should let Trevor go to Iceland alone and meet his mom in Ottawa ten days early, go to page 13, Chapter: Ottawa.

If you think Sean should do whatever it takes to convince Trevor to let him follow in his father's ill-fated footsteps to Iceland, keep reading on page 18, Chapter: Iceland Bound.

OTTAWA

Elizabeth knew something was wrong the minute she heard Sean's voice on the phone. She asked, "What do you mean your uncle doesn't want you?"

Sean sighed. "It's . . . complicated. He found . . . you see, there's this blip . . ."

At the lab, listening to Trevor babble, it had all made sense. But now, trying to explain the situation to his mother, Sean found himself at a loss for words.

"Why don't you put Trevor on the phone?" Elizabeth suggested.

Sean looked into the bedroom where Trevor pulled clothes off the closet floor and tossed them at his suitcase. "He's pretty busy packing for Iceland."

Elizabeth took a deep breath to keep herself from screaming. "Did you say Iceland?" she asked.

Sean wanted to blurt out, "He might find Dad!" But he knew that would only upset his mother. If she got really mad, Mom might even try to stop Trevor from trying to follow Max's trail. Instead Sean said, "It's okay, Mom, really. Uncle Trevor just . . . needs some time to do his work."

Elizabeth sighed. Science had torn Sean's father away from him, and now his uncle, too. And the last thing any teenager wants to feel is rejected. So she put on her most cheerful voice and chirped, "Well, that's Trevor's loss. I'll have my favorite helper on hand for the heavy boxes."

Elizabeth thought to herself, *And that's the last time I count on Uncle Trevor.*

By the time Sean and Elizabeth arranged when and where to meet in the Ottawa airport, Trevor had finished packing his suitcase. His flight left a few hours after Sean's. During the drive to the airport, neither knew what to say. Finally, Trevor apologized. "I'm really sorry to ruin our vacation together."

Sean shrugged. Like it mattered. He wasn't some pathetic kid needing attention. He had things to do, games to play, new friends to make in a new country.

Trevor added more softly, "This is probably the only chance we'll ever get to know what happened to your old man."

Sean sank deeper into his seat. That was all the more reason he should be going to Iceland, too. Sean muttered, "Yeah, don't forget to send me a postcard."

Trevor sighed. Sometimes it felt like no one understood him. Maybe that's why he missed Max so much. "Partners in crime," their mother had called them. More like brothers in science. Trevor had always believed that someday the Anderson brothers would be responsible for some great discovery or invention, like the Wright brothers. If he could prove his brother's theories correct, maybe Trevor could somehow make that dream come true. Or at least find out Max's fate and maybe end his own nightmares.

All the way to Iceland, Trevor puzzled over Max's copy of *Journey to the Center of the Earth*. But without Sean there to look at the notes from a fresh angle, Trevor never noticed that one seemingly nonsensical list of letters actually spelled Sigurbjörn Ásgeirsson, the name of the ill-fated scientist who shared Max's seismic concerns.

So instead of going directly to the Ásgeirsson Institute, Trevor stopped at a hotel. From there, he inquired about possible guides who could take him to Mount Snaeffels, the location of the seismic sensor and the entrance to the center of the Earth described in Verne's book.

The only guide in the area turned out to be Sigurbjörn Ásgeirsson's daughter, Hannah. But since Trevor arrived at the institute half a day later than he would have with Sean, Hannah refused to make the trip, because by then the front edge of a terrible storm had made its first appearance on the satellite map.

Trevor could not argue with the weather. "But I must retrieve that sensor!"

Hannah shook her head. "Professor, you have no idea how dangerous these storms can be. No sane guide would knowingly walk

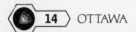

someone into such conditions."

Trevor's face turned red with frustration. "Then I'll find an insane guide!"

Hannah laughed quietly. She had seen this kind of obsession before, in her "brilliant" father, who had ended his days raving about Jules Verne in an asylum. All of her father's precious work wound up discredited because of his belief in a dead Frenchman's fiction. "There are no other guides in this part of the country. You can either wait until the storm passes, or go alone, which I do not recommend."

"What if I paid double your usual rate?" Trevor offered desperately, not even sure he could afford the guide's standard fee.

Hannah's bright blue eyes stared deeply into Trevor's. "You are stubborn, just like my father was, and you might learn something from his unfortunate example. No matter how smart you think you are, you cannot out-think a storm. You cannot win an argument with the wind. And most of all, you cannot persuade me to risk my life and yours for some scientific gadget, seismic reading, or anything else."

Trevor felt too frustrated to speak. Finally he managed to ask, "How long do you think the storm will last?"

Hannah shrugged. "Icelanders say, 'If you don't like the weather, wait a few minutes. It'll get worse.'"

Trevor managed a small chuckle. "I always heard that as 'it'll change.'"

Hannah smiled. "You haven't lived in Iceland."

While they waited for the storm to clear, Hannah and Trevor prepared for their trip. As long as he was careful not to mention anything Vernian, Trevor and the guide got along fine.

But they did not even set out for Mount Snaeffels until several days after the date mentioned in Verne's book. The first, or kalends, of July was the only time the sun struck at the right angle to point to the entrance to the center of the Earth.

So Trevor could not follow Max. He retrieved the seismic monitoring beacon and returned home. But, as usual, he could not find anyone who cared about the data.

After a while, Trevor stopped trying. He drifted further away from friends and family. Elizabeth and Sean never quite forgave him for the

"Iceland incident."

On the job, Trevor became one of those teachers who recites on automatic, instead of relating to his students. He didn't even try to help them feel the wonder of Earth's crust moving beneath them. Trevor just filed his paperwork and cashed his check.

When the university denied him tenure, Trevor took a job in construction. He found it oddly comforting to go to work in jeans and a T-shirt, to have his muscles feel exhausted at the end of the day instead of his spirits. The exercise and fresh air further lifted his mood, and day-to-day digging in the rocks rekindled his love of geology.

When Trevor started lecturing his lunch buddies about layers of rock, he realized he missed teaching. This time Trevor decided to try teaching younger students. He discovered elementary-school kids were far more interested in the world under their feet than gum-chewing college freshmen seemed to be.

These students loved Trevor's cartoons and models of crystals. Several of Trevor's pupils grew up to be giants in the field of plate tectonics. One young man named Randy even tried to find his way to the center of the Earth. Though unsuccessful, his exciting expedition led to many vital discoveries.

As he watched the TV movie based on Randy's adventure, Trevor felt mixed emotions. During the early part of the film, they showed Randy as a child. They even filmed a segment at the school where Trevor taught.

The actor playing Trevor dressed better than any teacher. He mispronounced Wegener, the name of the father of plate tectonics. But otherwise, Trevor had to admit the actor pretty much nailed his character on the head.

Trevor felt proud of Randy for his work in plate tectonics, and grateful for his help advancing Max's research and Verne's theories. But as the cameras went underground, farther than any man had ever gone, except perhaps Max, Trevor could not help feeling a twinge of regret.

What would have happened? What great adventure might have been if he and Sean had taken that journey? Trevor sighed. He had

not heard from Sean in several years. There had been the occasional postcard or phone call, then nothing. They both had their excuses. Sean had joined the military right out of high school. They paid for his education and gave him a chance to travel the world.

But no matter how many countries were stamped in his passport, Sean had only scratched the Earth's surface. He always wondered what might have happened if he'd dared to travel to the center of it with his uncle so long ago.

END.

To satisfy Sean's curiosity, keep reading on page 18, Chapter: Iceland Bound.

ICELAND BOUND

Sean yanked the phone's plug out of the wall. He stared at his uncle and said, "I just got here and you already want to ditch me? I'm the one who found your life's-work-fourth-blip in the first place."

Trevor didn't know how to make him understand. "Sean, he was my brother."

Sean's eyes burned with emotion. "He was my *father*! I don't have to be in Ottawa for ten days."

Trevor asked, "Do you know how much a last-minute flight to Iceland costs?"

Sean plugged the phone back in and nodded toward the four giant jars of coins. "I think you've got it covered."

The flight to Iceland gave Sean plenty of time to practice his yo-yo tricks and play his hand-held video games. Trevor studied Max's copy of *Journey to the Center of the Earth* intently. Sean asked, "What're you doing?"

Trevor explained. "Your old man drew all these notations that I can't decipher. I'm trying to decode this series of paired letters. Some of them are elements, like Rn, for example, I know is radon."

Sean glanced at the margin notes. Read normally, the letters seemed like nonsense. But Sean saw a legible pattern in the letters when read from top to bottom. He sounded out the strange word. "Sig . . . urb . . . jörn?"

Trevor thought he must have misheard. "I'm sorry?"

Sean took the book from his uncle. He ran his finger down the column of letters and struggled to pronounce the peculiar syllables. "Sigurbjörn Ásgeirsson? What's an Ásgeirsson? Is it a place, a password, some secret code?"

Trevor flipped through the book. On the last page, he saw the strange name again in his brother's neat handwriting above an address for the Ásgeirsson Institute for Progressive Volcanology.

Trevor felt another piece of the puzzle fall into place. "Max must have been in touch with him," he said, his voice rising with excitement. "Maybe this guy saw Max before he disappeared. I knew there was a reason I brought you, kid!"

But finding the Ásgeirsson Institute on the map proved much easier than driving there. Trevor had never seen a lonelier road. Though it was July in the land of the midnight sun, clouds dimmed the sky to a gloomy dusk. Trevor hoped the little compact rental car wouldn't break down. He couldn't remember the last time they'd seen a sign—or anything else for that matter! "You sure we're going the right way?" he asked.

"How should I know?" Sean said, looking at the map. "I can't read Icelandic. I, um, think there's just this one main highway."

The gray road stretched before them, between scrubby fields of frozen tundra under jagged mountains. What Iceland lacked in lush greenery or other bright colors, it made up for in the dramatic shapes of its pale peaks and the eerie emptiness of its tundra.

Sean broke the long silence to complain, "We've been driving forever." And then he asked the question every driver dreads. "Are we there yet?"

Trevor sighed. "No, we're not there yet."

A few more feet of flat tundra rolled past Sean's tired eyes. Sean stared into the thickening fog and asked, "Now?"

Trevor struggled to keep his temper. "No! Not now!"

Sean looked out the window again. Nothing had changed, except that the fog made the landscape seem even emptier. "You're driving kinda slow, man."

"I'm driving kinda safe," he responded.

"I just saw a goat in the passing lane," Sean teased. Then he could not stop himself from wondering, "When's the adventure part gonna begin?"

Trevor sighed. "Hey, we've been together a day and we're already in Iceland! What does it take with you kids these days?" The fog had swallowed up everything beyond the bumper. Trevor squinted, trying to stay on the road. "Anyway, the 'adventure part' begins when we find Sigurbjörn Ásgeirsson."

Though Sean did not believe it possible, the fog grew thicker. Trevor strained to see. "You'd think the Ásgeirsson Institute for Progressive Volcanology might have a couple of signs leading to it."

Sean looked out the windshield at the nothingness all around them. "How do you know we're not there right now? We could be in the parking lot for all we know."

Then, suddenly, *bang*! The car crashed into a sign emerging from the mist. The travelers read: THE ÁSGEIRSSON INSTITUTE FOR PROGRESSIVE VOLCANOLOGY.

The one-room roadside shack wasn't much bigger than its own sign. Sean wondered if this might be some kind of gatehouse, or maybe the entrance to a high-tech underground lab.

But his uncle recognized the shack as a humble outpost in the noble war against ignorance, one of science's many underfunded fortresses. Trevor smiled. "All righty. Not too shabby."

Sean shuddered. He never wanted to see his uncle's idea of shabby. They climbed the rickety steps. Then Trevor knocked on the door and shouted, "Sigurbjörn Ásgeirsson?! Hello?!"

From the other side of the thick door, Trevor and Sean heard a woman's muffled reply in Icelandic.

"I'm an American scientist looking for Sigurbjörn Ásgeirsson," Trevor shouted.

Sean shrugged at the reply, which was merely more muffled Icelandic.

Trevor kept talking to the wind-scarred wood. "I'm sorry, I don't speak Ice—"

The door swung open to reveal a young woman with long, blond hair and bright blue eyes. Trevor finished speaking, so as not to betray his cool. "—landic."

Sean stared at the beautiful woman, who seemed to be about Trevor's age.

"Can I help you?" she asked.

Trevor stammered in surprise. "You speak English."

"Yes, as well as French, Finnish, Croatian, and in a pinch, a little Farsi," the woman said as she reached out to shake Trevor's hand. "I'm Hannah."

"I'm Trevor Anderson, Professor of Tectonics, visiting from America with my nephew, uh . . ." Trevor felt so nervous he almost forgot his nephew's name.

Sean filled in the gap just as Trevor also said, "Sean. We're looking for Sigurbjörn Ásgeirsson."

Hannah's eyes dimmed. "Sigurbjörn Ásgeirsson is dead."

Sean did not want to believe they had come all this way for nothing. "Dead?"

Hannah nodded. "Three winters ago."

Trevor wondered how to proceed. "Did you work for him?"

Hannah stated simply, "He was my father."

"Oh. I'm sorry," Trevor said. "Who runs the institute?"

"There is no institute," Hannah declared. "Progressive Volcanology was a failed idea, like eight-track tapes." Her bright eyes narrowed to suspicious slits. "What business did you have with my father?"

Trevor did not want to spoil his chances for success by revealing too much right away. He wondered what sort of answer would be acceptable to the scientist's daughter. The awkward silence grew until Sean sniffed the air and remarked, "It sure smells good in there."

Hannah saw the boy shiver and realized she had been rude. She opened the door a little wider and said, "I was just stirring a pot of hot chocolate. Would you like some?"

Sean wanted the warm drink so much that he answered politely, "Yes, please."

Trevor and Sean both followed Hannah so eagerly that they nearly bumped heads in the narrow doorway. Sean's shoulder grazed one of the many loops of high-tech climbing ropes hanging from the cabin's heavy beams. The equipment made a faint clanking at the disturbance.

Soon they sat with steaming cocoa cups in their hands. Trevor passed Max's copy of *Journey to the Center of the Earth* across the rustic table to Hannah. Her curtain of golden hair prevented him from reading the expression in her shockingly blue eyes. She said flatly, "Yeah. I know it. What about it?"

Trevor explained, "This was my late brother's book. His name was

Max Anderson. And we believe he was in contact with your father."

Hannah's eyes narrowed. "Your brother was a Vernian?"

Sean had never heard that term. "What's a Vernian?"

Hannah replied, "A 'Vernian' is what I call members of La Société de Jules Verne, a group of fanatics who believe the writing of Jules Verne is actual fact." Her cool eyes flickered toward Trevor to see how he reacted as she went on. "I mean, the guy was a science *fiction* writer. But these believers regard him as a visionary. My father was the biggest Vernian of them all."

Hannah concluded with one simple, earnest declaration, "A Vernian is a fool."

Trevor did not want to get angry. But he said, "Well, my brother was no fool."

Hannah flipped through Max's much-scrawled-upon paperback. In reaction to his notes in the margin, she said, "Oh, yes, your brother was definitely a believer."

"He was?" Trevor asked.

"Big time. Check this out." Hannah walked across the tiny cabin to the bookshelf. She pulled out a hardcover, first edition copy of *Journey to the Center of the Earth.* "This was my father's." She handed the book to Trevor, who scanned the margin notes and numbers. The handwriting lacked Max's neatness and energy, but the figures, locations, and temperatures all matched, page for page. What did this mean?

Hannah regarded her uninvited guests. "Why are you two way out here? Are you Vernians?"

Trevor hastily replied, "Us? Vernians? Of course not."

For someone so pretty, Hannah looked quite tough as she added, "Good, because I do not suffer fools gladly."

Trevor spoke in a rush. "I'm a professor and a scientist. There's a seismic sensor going off just north of here that I think is worth checking on. That's why we've come out here."

Hannah figured he meant Mount Snaeffels, one of Iceland's most spectacular peaks and the key setting of Verne's book. "Well, I am a mountain guide. I will take you there, Professor," she agreed.

"So how much do you charge?" Trevor asked.

To reach the book's key location would not be an easy trip. "To go *there*?" Hannah replied. "Five thousand kronor."

Trevor struggled to calculate currency in his head. "A day?"

Hannah corrected him. "An hour."

Trevor whistled softly. "Steep rate."

Hannah's lips curled in a slow, sly smile. "It helps to be the only guide out here."

Sean didn't know a krona from a crack in the wall, but he knew his uncle's financial situation. "Do you accept rolls of quarters?"

Hannah would have taken pennies, if they added up to the correct amount. After some quick preparations, the guide and her two companions marched across the barren landscape toward the sensor's remote location. Trevor and Sean struggled to keep up with Hannah. Trevor shouted to Hannah, "Could you, ah, just slow down there by a degree?"

Sean gasped. "I don't think she can hear you. She's too far ahead." He stopped and doubled over to catch his breath.

Trevor turned to his tired nephew. "C'mon. Don't let her see you rest." Then he teased, "I thought you were this tough kid."

"In Orange, New Jersey, I'm tough," Sean wheezed. "In Iceland, I need oxygen."

Hannah's voice reached them on a gust of wind. "Move! I want to be home by sundown."

This was only an expression, since that far north in July, the sun stays up all night. Trevor and Sean knew what their guide meant, and their lungs didn't like the sound of it. But they pushed themselves to catch up to Hannah as the sky darkened with an oncoming storm, and the wind began to howl like a hungry wolf.

For a while it seemed like they made no progress toward the jagged peak. But eventually they reached a craggy crater atop Mount Snaeffels. Hannah asked, "Is your sensor in range?"

Trevor checked his GPS monitor. "Looks like we're getting close."

Hannah scanned the deserted crater and remarked, "Before the mines caved in, Snaeffels was once very busy."

"What's Snaeffels?" Sean asked.

"This peak," Hannah replied.

"Snaeffels is the mountain in Verne's ridiculous science *fiction* book where this character named Lidenbrock *supposedly* found this portal to the center of the Earth," Trevor said.

But Hannah wondered if he only recited what she wanted to hear. Hannah decided to stick to business. "Let's just find that sensor of yours, Professor. The weather is turning."

"Yeah, yeah . . . give me a minute to catch my breath," Trevor said, staring around him at the various peaks poking at the darkening sky. He could not help feeling awestruck to be standing on the very mountain in Verne's amazing book.

Hannah shivered impatiently. "We must get going. I do not like it up here, especially on the kalends."

Trevor jumped at the strange, old-fashioned word. "Did you say 'the kalends'?"

Hannah hiked on. "Yes, today is July first, the kalends of July. But you wouldn't know that would you, Professor? Because you're not a Vernian, right?"

Trevor did not hear her, because he was lingering behind at the crater, mumbling a passage from *Journey to the Center of the Earth* that he remembered by heart, ". . . in the crater of the Jokul of Snaeffels when the shadow of Scartaris touches, at the kalends of July you will attain the center of the Earth . . ." Trevor swallowed hard. He still could not believe where he stood and on what date.

Sean shouted from a nearby ridge. "Trevor! Your sensor! I think I see it!"

Trevor ran up to join Sean. The sensor's red light still blinked. Trevor's hands shook with excitement and cold as he tried to insert a key into the rusty device.

Hannah asked, "What are you doing with it?"

Trevor grunted with frustrated effort. "Trying to disengage the cylinder . . . the entire seismic history of the last decade is locked inside. If I download the black box, the readings might tell me what kind of activity happened when Max was here."

Sean blinked in the growing darkness. He felt as if he'd suddenly put on sunglasses.

Hannah felt the wind gaining energy, whipping itself up for one of Iceland's notoriously nasty sudden storms. She asked, "How long is this going to take? The weather is turning. We have to go back. I'm sorry, Trevor."

Without stopping his effort to release the sensor, Trevor replied, "Hard to tell. There's a lot of rust."

Before he could go on, a massive boom of thunder shook the ground. The jolt rattled all three from their teeth to their toes. Not even Hannah had ever felt such a large clap so close.

Hannah shouted, "Trevor! We need to take cover!" Her expert eyes quickly spotted a suitable cave. She grabbed Sean's hand and shouted over the wild wind. "Come on, Sean!"

Trevor stubbornly struggled with the sensor, even as more thunder boomed above him. Then the black clouds began pouring a river of rain. Trevor shouted, "I've almost got it! Just another minute!"

Hannah had no patience with obsessed scientists. How could such a smart man not even have the sense to get out of the storm? Hannah shivered from the rain drying on her face. She muttered to herself, "He's as crazy as my father was . . ."

Sean watched his uncle, a dark, desperate figure outlined in flashes of lightning that were frighteningly near. Rain soaked Trevor's hair and clothing as he gave the sensor one more powerful tug. Trevor almost fell over as the device finally pulled free of the ground. He shouted triumphantly, "Got it!" and waved the sensor over his head.

Lightning tore through the sky toward Trevor with a loud crack and a startling flash way too close for comfort. Sean shouted, "Uncle Trevor!"

Hannah commanded, "Get in here!"

Trevor quickly recovered his cool. "I'm fine."

Crack! Another lightning bolt landed even closer. Hannah suddenly understood the cause of the danger. "Drop the sensor!"

But Trevor did not hear Hannah over the raging storm. A third bolt hit the ground right beside the scientist. Trevor clutched his precious prize as he ran for the cave. Deadly bolts of shining volts chased him like the arrows of an angry god.

Hannah shouted at the top of her lungs. "DROP IT! DROP THE SENSOR!"

Still unable to hear her over the thunder shaking the whole mountaintop, Trevor just kept running toward the cave. Seeking the sensor's electrical energy, the lightning tracked Trevor to the cave. *Boom!* Just as he entered, a bolt zapped the entrance.

Huge rocks crashed to the cave floor and the opening completely collapsed! Trevor called into the sudden darkness. Shocked but unhurt, Sean answered his uncle. Hannah replied by switching on a flashlight. By its bright beam, they saw the seriousness of their situation.

After briefly trying to budge the massive heap of rocks, Hannah concluded, "Forget it. It's no use."

Sean's panic deepened. "What do you mean, 'forget it'?"

Trevor sighed. "She's right. There must be sixty tons of rock here. It would take us months to dig out. We'll have to find another way."

Fear held Sean tightly now. "What if there's not 'another way'?!"

"We should look around," Hannah said. "Most caves have several openings."

Sean stared into the horrible darkness beyond their tiny circle of light. "Maybe we should stay here. At least near the entrance we stand a chance of rescue."

If you want to stay near the surface with Sean, keep reading on page 27, Chapter: Surface.

If you want to explore other ways out of the cave, continue on page 49, Chapter: Caves.

SURFACE

Hannah and Trevor searched their gear for a means of moving all those rocks. Hannah passed out the headlamps she kept in her bag so that they could see. Sean waited impatiently as they discussed various possibilities.

"We might be able to rig some kind of explosive using the flares," Hannah suggested.

Trevor agreed. "But how could we be sure it would pack enough punch?"

Hannah shrugged and looked worried. "I'm more concerned about creating too much punch in this confined space." Her eyes flickered toward Sean.

Trevor nodded.

Sean said. "What do you mean?"

Hannah opened her mouth but said nothing. For a young person who had probably never been in a life-threatening situation before, Sean held himself together pretty well. But she did not want to have to cope with his emotions once they seized on all the grim fates that might figure into their future.

Sean's headlamp swept over the cave and his companions' worried faces. "I get it. Don't scare the kid. If we use too many explosives we might blow ourselves up with the rocks. Is that right?" he demanded.

Trevor sighed and wondered how parents manage. It's one thing to cajole a tense toddler, but how did you soothe a teenager with a perfectly sound reason to freak out?

As he tried to come up with the right thing to say, Trevor's headlamp lit a strange stripe in the cave wall. "It's more likely that our explosion will be too feeble to be dangerous, unless . . ." Trevor's voice trailed off as he stared at the odd stripe.

Hannah frowned. "This is no time to study rocks, Professor."

Trevor took a small knife out of his pocket and scraped a few flakes from the shiny stripe. "It's the perfect time—if this turns out to be what I think it is."

Trevor put the shiny flakes on a flat rock. Then he asked Hannah, "Do you have a match?"

The guide's only answer was the near-instant extraction of a matchbox from her pile of gear.

Trevor smiled, then bowed his head and announced, "Lady and gentleman, for his next trick, Trevor the Terrific proudly presents . . ." Trevor struck a match on the side of the box and touched its flame to the flakes. After a bright flash of white fire, Trevor concluded, ". . . magnesium! Everyone's favorite element, or at least it's certainly one of mine."

Hannah grinned. "You're all right, Professor! Add some of your magic magnesium to my flares and we just might blow ourselves out of here."

Sean raised both fists in the air and shouted, "Yahoo! Three cheers for outta here!"

But then Trevor spoiled the jubilant mood with a serious question. "Should we use all four flares at once, or try one first?"

If you think they should use all four flares, keep reading on page 29, Chapter: Four Flares.

If you think they should start with one flare, keep reading on page 34, Chapter: One Flare.

FOUR FLARES

While Trevor and Hannah prepared the bomb, Sean paced the small space, trying to calm down. In a few minutes they would either be free or . . .

Sean shuddered. His vivid imagination briefly considered the not-so-happy outcomes that might result from their situation. What would it feel like to fly through the air, propelled by a bomb?

Trevor looked up from the handmade explosive, catching Sean's worried expression. Trevor said, "It'll be all right, Sean!" with more conviction than he felt.

Sean gave his uncle the thumbs-up sign.

Hannah stood up and wiped her hands on her pants. She could not think of anything to say. What was the proper expression for we-might-die-any-minute-but-here's-hoping-we-don't? Hannah met Trevor and Sean's nervous gazes. She smiled briefly and shrugged. Then she muttered something in Icelandic, which she quickly translated as "Good luck."

Trevor put a hand on each of their shoulders and said, "Okay, let's do this thing!" Then he added, "Once you guys are down that passage a little way, I'll light the things and come running."

Hannah shook her head. "We stay together."

Trevor started to protest. "But I . . ."

Hannah held up her hand. "If there's another cave-in, I'd rather not be alone. Whatever happens, let's see it through together."

Trevor blinked, not knowing how to counter Hannah's argument.

"Okay," he finally said. "We do this together."

They stood near the bomb. Trevor struck another match.

"Get ready to run!" he said. Then he touched the little yellow flame to one of the fuses.

After a tense second, just long enough for Trevor to worry that the flares might be duds, the fuse sparked to life, giving off a powerful, red glow. He quickly touched the match to the other fuses and cried, "Go, go, go!"

The three travelers ran for the passage at the back of the cave just as the magnesium caught with a startling flash many times brighter than the most obnoxious camera.

Trevor, Hannah, and Sean kept running, even though they couldn't see or hear anything.

In the eerie silence following the loud explosion, Sean felt the frantic beating of his heart. His legs moved, but he heard no footfalls. Sean felt Trevor's hand tugging him forward. Then he stumbled, and pain reached his brain from two badly skinned knees.

Hannah's hands found Sean's shoulders. She shouted, "Sean? Are you okay?"

Hannah's voice reached Sean faintly, as if his ears were clogged with cotton. She seemed to be having a hard time hearing, too. Sean considered her question. "I . . . my knees hurt," he shouted. "But I think I'm okay."

Hannah replied, "Your bees hurt?"

Her hands explored Sean's face, feeling for signs of injury.

Sean smirked. "My KNEES!" he screamed.

Hannah shouted back, "Oh! KNEES. What about you, Trevor?"

As she fished through her pack for the first aid kit, Hannah waited tensely for an answer.

"I'm OKAY!" Trevor lied at the top of his lungs. "I . . ." Trevor told himself the condition must be temporary. "I'm blind!"

Hannah shouted, "What?"

Trevor repeated, "Blind! I'm blind!"

Hannah exclaimed, "Oh my goodness! I assumed our headlamps had gone out." She flipped the switch on hers and it made no difference. Hannah blinked and saw no more with her eyes open than with them closed.

Sean heard only bits and pieces of Hannah's words. He shouted in frustration, "What? What did you say?"

"It must be temporary!" Hannah agreed. But, like Trevor, she expressed a hope more than a certainty.

"You guys can't see, either?" Sean yelled.

Trevor nodded, then realized gestures meant nothing to the blind. "Probably a temporary result of the bright magnesium flash."

Sean panicked. "How do you know? We could be like this for the rest of our lives!"

Trevor followed the sound of Sean's voice until he could put his arm around his nephew. "Don't assume the worst," Trevor said into Sean's ear. "Let's see if that bomb did its job."

Sean shuddered. Would they ever see anything again?

Hannah wanted to patch up Sean's knees first, but Trevor needed to know if they were still trapped or free. Holding hands, the three travelers slowly made their way back to the cave opening. "Look out for rubble," Hannah cautioned.

They could still hear the faint sound of dust and debris settling to the cave floor. As soon as they cleared the passageway back to the main chamber, Trevor felt a cool breeze on his skin. He rushed forward impatiently to find out if they would need to dig or if the blast hole would be big enough to walk through.

Hannah's shaking hands explored a gap large enough for all three explorers to walk through side by side. "We're free!" she shouted, enjoying a big lungful of fresh, Icelandic air.

Sean stepped through the gap, rejoicing in the rain drenching his head, because it meant freedom.

Despite the storm, Sean's cell phone managed to connect with the Icelandic rescue service. While they waited in the cave, Hannah tended to Sean's knees. Since she knew the contents of her first aid kit well, Hannah did not have much trouble finding antiseptic wipes and bandages the right size to cover his wounds.

In less than an hour, all three received expert medical attention when the rescue helicopter touched down on Mount Snaeffels. The paramedics could not confirm whether their sight would return.

"We'll know more when you get to the hospital," one medic explained as he strapped Sean into his seat.

Despite the closeness of the roaring engine and whirring propellers, Sean only heard these loud sounds dimly. He felt the copter lift off and thought wistfully, *I bet there's a great view!*

Hearing returned before sight. But the travelers still talked loudly or several days. Elizabeth dropped everything and flew out to Iceland to be with Sean and Trevor in the hospital. Within a week, their blurry vision showed signs of healing completely.

On the night before their flight back to the United States, Elizabeth took the three adventurers out for a fancy dinner in Reykjavík, Iceland's capital city. She raised her glass and toasted, "Here's looking at you—and to you being able to see me!"

Trevor tapped Elizabeth's glass with his. "I'll drink to that."

Sean sipped his soda thoughtfully. The young man's time unable to see had changed him. Sean announced, "I've decided to study blindness when I grow up. I think I can come up with ways to cure it, or at least help people cope with it better."

Elizabeth couldn't have been more proud. Before his Icelandic adventure, her son had been drifting. Now he seemed so mature, full of a purpose larger than just having fun. Elizabeth smiled. "Your grandma always said that every cloud has a silver lining."

Trevor remarked, "Seems like being blind for a while helped you see your path."

Sean agreed. "Yeah, that feels pretty good." Then he turned to Hannah and asked, "What about you?"

The pretty guide looked down at the butter plate and blushed. "I . . . don't know," Hannah confessed. "I've been a guide most of my adult life," she explained. "I've guided others, but I've never really followed my own path."

Trevor asked, "Well, what do you want to do?"

Hannah blushed more deeply before admitting, "I'd like to do something to help my country—even the world. But what can I do?" Hannah's blue eyes sought Trevor's, before looking away shyly. "I envy your sense of mission, Professor."

Trevor laughed bitterly. "All this mission has gotten me so far is frustration!" Then he added, "Oh, and got us all stuck in a cave and temporarily blinded."

"But if I had your scientific knowledge . . ." Hannah began.

"What would you do?" Trevor asked.

Hannah's blue eyes brightened. "Don't you see? The very geothermic disturbances your brother warned against might turn

Iceland into the next source for renewable, clean, affordable energy."

Trevor thumped the table excitedly, rattling silverware. "Why didn't I think of this before?" he demanded. "If we could divert the energy built up by the seismic cycle . . ."

Hannah smiled. "It could work, right?"

Trevor pulled a small notebook out of his pocket and scribbled a diagram while muttering, "A network of subterranean tunnels, criss-crossing like the natural ones described by Verne . . ."

Hannah offered, "I can contact the Icelandic government. If we can demonstrate the economic benefits, we might be able to get some kind of development grant. Geothermal plants already heat nine out of ten Icelandic homes. But this would increase production to export-able levels."

Elizabeth picked up her menu, then told Sean, "I hope you like it here. Because I think we'll be visiting your Uncle Trevor and Hannah in Iceland from now on."

Trevor looked from Elizabeth to Hannah, whose beautiful blue eyes seemed to glow. Trevor grinned, "Well, it is the most geothermically exciting place on the planet! Where else can you experience an average of thirty-three earthquakes in a day?"

Sean laughed. "Uncle Trevor, you are such a nerd!"

Within a year, Trevor and Hannah had both a government grant and a prototype. Within five, they had created a multinational energy company that produced pollution-free fuel while preventing volcanic eruptions.

When Trevor got the call from a news magazine telling him he'd been named "Achiever of the Year," he thought Sean had rigged a practical joke. But the honor turned out to be real!

In his interview, Trevor gave Hannah credit for helping him see the practical side of plate tectonics. He also thanked Dean Kitzens for kicking him out of the lab, which propelled him up to Iceland for the journey of a lifetime!

END.

ONE FLARE

Trevor lit the fuse and the flare sparked to glowing, red life. Then the magnesium ignited and . . . *FLASH! BOOM!*

Rocks clattered to the cave floor. Dust blew through the air. But when it settled, the travelers saw that the rock wall remained intact.

Sean said, "Maybe we should have used all four flares."

"We could set off the remaining three at once," Trevor suggested.

"What if that doesn't work?" Hannah asked.

Sean spotted Hannah's climber's pick. "Can't we break up rocks with that? Maybe we can dig our way out. The explosion probably thinned the wall some."

Trevor took another look at the explosion site. Some rocks had been blasted away. Perhaps they had created a thin spot. But would it be thin enough to break through with a climber's pick?

If you think they should explode the three remaining flares, keep reading on page 35, Chapter: Three Flares.

If you think they should try digging, keep reading on page 38, Chapter: Dig.

THREE FLARES

Trevor chipped off more magnesium flakes, then topped the pile with a bundle of the three remaining flares. He took a deep breath and turned to the others. "As soon as I light it, take cover!"

Sean turned his back to the bomb and bent over to cover his head.

The magnesium flashed and the flares boomed!

Then something slapped Sean right in the back pocket. "Ow!" he exclaimed. Then he reached in his pocket and pulled out his shattered cell phone.

Trevor whistled softly, "That, my friend, could have been your butt."

Hannah said, "Must have been a piece of rock loosened by the explosion. You're lucky indeed!"

Sean didn't feel lucky when he realized that without that phone to summon help, the three faced a long, difficult trek back to civilization through what continued to be a fierce storm. But at least the three-flare bomb had done the job. Sean looked out at the pouring rain.

"We can wait for it to pass," Hannah offered. "But the storm might go on for several days."

Sean's stomach growled. "What about food?"

Hannah said, "We're more likely to find edibles out there than in the cave."

Sean liked the idea of getting out of the cave, even if rain continued to drench the outside world. He said, "Okay, let's get started."

Hannah smiled. "Good. You'll see. We'll manage."

The trek down Mount Snaeffels through the storm was no Sunday hike. But during that difficult descent, Sean learned how to build a shelter in the wild and how to track, trap, and cook small game.

Reindeer moss filled their bellies, even if it didn't provide much nutrition. Sean wondered, "Why is it called reindeer moss?"

Hannah held up a piece of the scrubby, off-white moss that covered so many rocks in the region. "These branches look like tiny antlers," the guide explained.

Sean picked another bunch and looked at the moss before popping it into his mouth. "Yeah, I see it now. Too bad it doesn't taste like barbecued reindeer."

"You've eaten barbecued reindeer?" Trevor teased.

Sean replied around a mouthful of moss. "No, but I'd like to!"

When they returned to civilization, Sean surprised himself by feeling just a little disappointed. Life in the wild had an edge that no computer game could ever match.

Sean traded his hand-held video game console for camping gear. He became a survival expert, taking many people into deep wilderness for the first time. Sean often shared with them the story of his own awakening to the thrill of survival one stormy summer on Mount Snaeffels.

The trek down the mountain had a similar effect on Trevor, reminding him of how much he missed the grit-under-your-finger-nails fun of field geology. Giving Dean Kitzens his notice felt pretty fun, too. Best of all, Trevor discovered that he could make lots of money hunting for rare gemstones while discovering some fascinating fossils.

But without the Maxwell Anderson lab monitoring certain subterranean activities, Earth suffered from the disasters Max had hoped to avert. Earthquakes and violent volcanoes wiped out entire islands, taking thousands of lives and leaving millions homeless.

Trevor felt torn by guilt. If he had reached the center of the Earth . . . If only he had been able to prove the rising danger warned of by the blips . . . Could all those people have been spared? If only he could have convinced someone that Max was right.

While on business in Iceland, Trevor visited Hannah. To his amazement, not even the mega-disasters predicted by Max's blips convinced her of the truth behind his "Vernian" theories.

"But surely now that all this has happened . . ." Trevor began.

Hannah reached the limit of her patience. She said, "I wish you would stop mentioning Jules Verne in my presence. His science-less fiction should be condemned as an encyclopedia for fools!"

Trevor took offense at being indirectly called a fool. And before either of them knew it, the door slammed on their friendship forever.

END.

DIG

Trevor, Sean, and Hannah took turns assaulting the wall with the climber's ax.

"Swing it over your head," Trevor instructed. "Let gravity give it extra strength."

Sean rubbed his sore hands on his thighs. It seemed like they'd been hacking at the rocks for hours, without so much as a glimmer of daylight. Red blisters blossomed on Sean's palms. His shoulders and back ached. Thirst and hunger constantly nagged him. But worst of all, Sean suffered from the fear that their situation would only get worse.

Trevor saw his nephew's weary expression. "Take five," he told the teenager. "It's my turn to work my muscles." Trevor flexed his arms like a championship wrestler.

While Trevor whacked at the wall, Sean flipped open his cell phone. Trying to get a signal gave him something to do—besides worrying.

At the sound of the phone bleeping to life, Trevor glanced over at Sean. "Give it up," Trevor advised. "Don't waste the battery. We might be able to use it for something."

Sean knew his uncle made a good point. But he felt a strong instinct to try one more time.

If you think Sean should try the call, keep reading on page 39, Chapter: Call.

If you think Sean should listen to his uncle, keep reading on page 44, Chapter: Keep Digging.

CALL

Sean glanced at the phone in disbelief. Somehow it had acquired a signal! He asked Hannah, "What's Icelandic for 911?"

"Dial 112," the guide replied.

Sean saw the tiny, glowing screen report "Dialing," then "Connected." He hastily handed the phone to Hannah.

The guide gave a clear description of their location and situation. She even heard confirmation that help was on the way before the miraculous signal went dead, along with Sean's battery.

"They got our location?" Trevor asked.

Hannah nodded. "Not precisely, but they know we're on the mountain."

Sean shouted, "Awesome!"

Hannah cautioned. "We can't count on rescue to arrive right away. Mount Snaeffels is a big mountain to search, especially in a storm."

Time passed extremely slowly in the dark cave. Since they could not be sure of when, or even if, rescue would arrive, the travelers conserved their limited resources of water, food, and energy.

Fear tiptoed up to Sean over and over again, like a mouse nibbling at his courage. How long would it take to die of hunger and thirst? What if lightning struck the cave again, crushing them under all these rocks?

Trevor's mind wandered outside the cave to the problems he would face back home and on the job. *"If I live through this,"* Trevor promised himself, *"I'm going to spend less time moping and more coping."*

Hannah's two protein bars did not go a long way toward keeping up the travelers' strength. "I should've carried an entire case of bars," the guide chided herself. Hannah had taken many precautions in her preparations for the trip. But a parade of missed opportunities to do better marched across her mind during those horrible dark hours.

Trevor tried to console her. "Coulda, woulda, shoulda."

The Icelander asked, "What's that supposed to mean?"

Trevor apologized for using slang. "Sorry. It's short for 'could have, would have, should have.' And it means, don't beat yourself up over things in the past."

Hannah grumbled, "Easier to say when you are the professor, not the professional guide. Your safety was in my hands and I . . ." Hannah trailed off when she saw Sean's frightened expression. She added brightly, "I'm just sorry I didn't pack us a better picnic."

Trevor chuckled. "You are forgiven. But for future reference, please remember that I like egg salad." Trevor hoped that Sean would join in their feeble joking. His nephew's silence seemed ominous. "Sean, are you all right?"

"Peachy keen," the teenager snapped. Then he laughed nervously. "Sorry, guys. I'm just a little jumpy." The word did not begin to describe the cold, damp horror seeping into Sean's heart. In the small voice of a scared child, Sean asked, "Are we gonna die?"

Trevor chuckled and put his arm around Sean. "I've been in tighter spots than this. Why, one time Max and I . . ."

Trevor saw a worried look cross Sean's face at the mention of his father. "Bad example," Trevor added quickly. "Um, all I'm saying is, we're not hanging over the edge of a cliff. We still have some water, and I bet we'll get rescued any minute."

"You bet, but you don't know," Sean replied.

Trevor shrugged. "You're right. We can't know. And the older you get, the more you'll realize how uncertain everything is."

"Gee, thanks!" Sean teased.

"But it's okay," Hannah chimed in. "You get used to it. And you learn that you can handle whatever comes up because . . . you have to."

Sean burst out laughing. "Promise me you guys will never go on talk radio."

Hannah and Trevor laughed, too, and it felt so good they all just kept laughing, until Sean heard a rhythmic *whup-whup-whup.*

Hannah grinned. "The rescue chopper!"

The three travelers shouted as loud as they could. And soon rescue workers shouted back. Hannah translated from the Icelandic. "We need to step back and cover our heads. They're going to use explosives."

KA-BOOM!

Sean blinked like a mole in the sudden light of the Icelandic summer night. "We're alive!" He tilted his face up to the open sky and added joyfully, "We're free!"

Trevor turned to Hannah and said, "Lady, you owe me an egg salad sandwich."

Hannah laughed. "I'll buy it with the hourly fee you owe me!"

When they said good-bye at the airport, Hannah told Trevor, "Keep in touch."

Trevor looked deep into her bright blue eyes and said, "Thanks, I will!"

Later, as the plane rose into the air, Trevor thought of Hannah's words, and the promise he had made to himself to change. "Keep in touch," the scientist muttered to himself. Then he would have jumped out of his seat, if his seatbelt hadn't stopped him.

"What is it?" Sean asked.

"I'll get in touch with everyone else who's trying to save the planet!" Trevor gushed. "I've been trying to go it alone, thinking only of my specialty, plate tectonics, and the seismic dangers threatening Earth."

"So?" Sean wondered.

"I'm not the only one who loves this planet," Trevor began. "If I get in touch with every group trying to save Earth, and if we all work together . . ." Trevor's voice trailed off as he picked up his notebook and started scribbling.

"Nice talking to you, too," Sean said sarcastically.

Trevor grinned sheepishly. "Sorry, Sean. I'm having a 'eureka' moment."

Sean smiled back. "That's okay. I'll let you get back to it."

"Thanks," Trevor said. And in seconds, he started scribbling with renewed fervor.

Sean looked at his uncle and recalled the laugh they shared with Hannah just before the helicopter arrived. Then he had his own "eureka" moment and started scribbling, too.

Sean had always admired stand-up comics. But he'd been too scared to get up in front of an audience. Sean remembered Trevor saying, "We're not hanging off the edge of a cliff." Since bombing at stand-up wouldn't kill him, Sean decided to give it a try. He wrote about being scared out of his wits in the cave. He exaggerated it, and made himself into even more of a jerk. Sean burst out laughing.

Trevor turned and asked, "What's so funny?"

Sean handed him the piece of paper entitled, "Things That Aren't So Funny in the Dark." Trevor read silently for a little while, then burst out laughing, too. "This is good!"

Sean grinned. "I know! And now I'm almost looking forward to going to a new school in a new country. It'll make great material."

Trevor looked at Sean warily. "Are you going to make fun of me, too?"

Sean smiled. "Only the funny parts!"

Almost as soon as the plane touched down, Trevor began his campaign of getting in touch with every Earth-friendly organization on the planet. He alerted them all to the seismic dangers Max's research revealed.

He attended conferences and educated volunteers. Trevor stopped waiting for the university or anyone else to help him. He rolled up his sleeves and told anyone who would listen, "If we all work together, we can save the world."

Other leaders saw the sense in Trevor's plea and suggested creating a worldwide volunteer organization similar to the Peace Corps but dedicated to the study, protection, and preservation of the Earth.

Earth Corps volunteers did great things all over the planet, including restoring Max's system of seismic sensors. As the data poured in from "Blip Brigades" worldwide, Trevor analyzed and predicted enormous ecological disasters. Thanks to the facts and figures gathered by the volunteers, other scientists confirmed Trevor's conclusions.

Whole cities evacuated based on what the blips revealed about the movements of the titanic forces seething under the Earth's crust. Politicians argued over the cost—until the disaster struck exactly when, where, and as severely as Trevor predicted. Millions of people owed their lives to Trevor's blips.

Sean told him, "Dude, you are a no-brainer to win the Nobel Prize." Then he added more quietly, "My dad would be so proud!"

Trevor, of course, gave credit to Max when he did eventually accept a Nobel Prize. "This really should go to the Anderson brothers," he said. Trevor recalled Max's scrapbook. "We've come a long way from blowing up the school chemistry lab. I only wish Max could be here now to share this moment."

Everyone cheered.

Later, reporters crowded around, asking Trevor, "What are you going to do now?"

Trevor said, "I'm not sure."

"I bet you could use a vacation," one reporter remarked.

"That'd be great!" Trevor replied. "A theme park, a beach, anywhere." Then he thought of one vacation completely lacking in appeal. "Just don't take me spelunking."

Several reporters chuckled. But Trevor never walked into a cave again. Sean did, but only on the set of his hit comedy show, *Laughing in the Dark.* By the time the special aired on Canadian TV, Sean had written and performed many routines. But he always included his signature "cave bit," which critics called "both funny and real."

Hannah's time in the cave inspired her to go even more deeply into survival training. After a while, the student learned so much that she knew more than her teachers. Hannah wound up starting a survival school and training the people who trained Navy Seals. The school's motto: Prepare to Survive!

END.

KEEP DIGGING

Working in shifts, the three determined travelers just kept picking away at the rocks robbing them of their freedom. Hannah's protein bars did not make for much of a meal. After that, they rationed their water and fought the rocks for as long as they could stand.

Since no sunlight penetrated their prison, they relied on their watches to tell day from night. After two days, Sean's stomach growled like a hungry bear. His eyes looked sunken and his hands shook. The teenager's growing body could not last without fuel.

"Try to sleep," Hannah advised.

Sean tried, but his growling gut gave him no peace. Hannah suggested, "We should go look for food and water."

Sean wondered, "What kind of food could we find in a cave?"

Trevor tried to lighten the mood. "Something pale, blind, and wiggly."

Hannah shook her head. "We're not in deep enough to find true troglobites."

Puzzling over the strange word distracted Sean from his hunger. "Troglo-whats?"

"*Troglo* is Greek for cave or hole," Trevor explained. "Troglobites are animals adapted to living only in caves. They're often colorless and blind or even eyeless."

Hannah added, "Unless we go deeper, we're more likely to find trogloxenes or troglophiles."

Sean protested, "Okay, now you guys are just showing off."

"Trogloxenes are cave 'guests,'" Hannah explained. "Like the bats and rats who sometimes roost and nest in caves. But there are no bats in Iceland."

Sean smirked. "Okay, so we'll eat rats."

"If we're lucky enough to find any," Trevor said.

Sean hoped for something tastier. "What about that other troglo-thingy?"

Hannah replied, "Troglophiles are creatures that love caves, like crickets, beetles, snails, worms, and spiders."

Sean groaned. "You're really making my mouth water."

Trevor put his arm around his nephew's shoulder and teased, "How can you know you don't like something until you've tried it?"

Sean's stomach growled. "Fine. Let's go hunting!"

"That's the spirit!" Trevor declared.

Hannah pulled out her knife and said, "I'll blaze our trail so we can find our way back here." Then they set off to explore the cave.

For a long time they saw only rocks. Then suddenly, something squeaked and Sean turned just in time to see a mouse running along the tunnel floor.

"Follow it!" Hannah exclaimed. "The mouse may know a way out."

They chased the mouse up a twisting tunnel. Then the mouse disappeared into a wall. Sean blinked. "Where did it go?"

Hannah bent down and examined the base of the wall. "I smell fresh air!"

Trevor found the tiny chink in the wall with his fingers. "Maybe this little guy has shown us a better place to dig."

"That's great, but I'm still hungry," Sean pointed out.

Hannah shone her headlamp all around. She stopped when it fell upon a small patch of straw. In it a mother mouse nursed a nest full of wiggling, pink babies.

Sean gagged at the thought of eating anything that cute. But Trevor had a better idea. "Don't mice store food in their nests?"

Hannah gently lifted some of the straw and found a "pantry" full of seeds and berries. She handed these precious morsels to her companions. They all chewed slowly.

"I bet we can find a few other mouse nests," Trevor suggested.

"Yeah, before we get desperate enough to eat Minnie and friends," Sean agreed.

Thanks to the tiny chink in the wall, that part of the cave was indeed home to many mouse nests. The travelers soon found whole handfuls of nutritious seeds. The fresh air also gave them hope of soon being able to dig their way out.

With his belly closer to full than it had been in days, Sean yawned, "I think I could actually sleep now."

"Let's all sleep and then start digging fresh," Trevor suggested. "Hopefully our little friends will restock their pantries."

As they drifted into sleep, Trevor's mind wandered to the book that had brought them to this strange fate. Just as the feverish, starving character in Verne's adventure imagines battles between prehistoric beasts, Trevor pictured huge lizards locked in combat, leathery tails lashing, giant jaws snapping in savage fury.

Hannah drifted to a much more pleasant place—Paris. During her student years, Hannah had fallen in love with the City of Lights, and ever after had always longed to return. In her mind, Hannah strolled the banks of the Seine, climbed the Eiffel Tower, and filled her eyes with art at the Louvre.

Sean imagined being rescued by his mom. He did not know how Elizabeth would find him. But he believed that somehow she would!

Sean remembered getting stuck in a trunk while playing hide-and-seek at a very young age. Sean had slipped into the old trunk in his friend's shed, but couldn't open it from the inside. He'd screamed himself hoarse, but no one had heard him, and then, exhausted, Sean had fallen sleep.

His friend assumed Sean was playing a trick and walked home. When it got dark, Elizabeth had called the friend's mother wondering why Sean was so late.

Sean woke to the sound of his mother's voice calling his name. He never forgot the pure joy they shared on seeing each other again. In the dark cave, Sean clung to that joy and the hope that somehow he might feel it again.

Sure enough, Elizabeth Anderson's mothering instincts went into overdrive when she couldn't reach Sean on his cell and no one answered Trevor's landline. The police tracked Trevor's credit card trail to Iceland. The car rental clerk recalled Trevor and Sean buying a map and asking about the Ásgeirsson Institute.

Like any good guide, Hannah had left a record of her expedition at the institute. Her notes led the rescue team to the seismic sensor's site. At the crater, the crew recognized the signs of a recent cave-in. They blasted through the rocks, then followed Hannah's knife marks to the cave full of mouse nests.

Sean thought he was still dreaming when he heard his mother's voice cry, "Sean!" But when Elizabeth hugged him, Sean's eyes fluttered open. Confused, but so happy, he murmured, "Mom?"

"Yes!" Elizabeth exclaimed. "It's me. I found you!"

Sean recognized the look of pure joy in his mother's eyes, and he knew she was also remembering that night in his friend's shed. "I knew you would," Sean said weakly.

Trevor gave such charming interviews about their adventure that he soon became the host of a TV show called *Finding the Facts Behind Fiction*. His celebrity helped him fund a much better Maxwell Anderson Institute for Plate Tectonics.

With state-of-the-art equipment, Trevor eventually proved his brother's theories and his own worth as a serious scientist. But to his chagrin, for the rest of his life, strangers always recognized Trevor as "that TV guy who was too nice to eat mice." In his later years, this reputation landed Trevor a lucrative infomercial job selling the Mouse Mansion, a super system of modular shelters and toys for pet mice, complete with "cars" and water fountains.

After his hungry time in the cave, Sean felt more grateful for everyday things. It's not that he stopped getting angry at his mom, but he became more inclined to stop and think before saying something snarky.

Elizabeth appreciated the change in her son. One night on the phone to Trevor, she struggled to describe it. "Since the cave, Sean's more . . . mature sounds too stuffy. I guess it's compassionate."

Trevor laughed. "Well, he didn't learn anything from me, except the names of various rocks."

Elizabeth laughed, too. "Maybe I should be thanking the mice."

After their return to civilization, Sean became a vegetarian. Since meatless meals helped her stick to her budget, Elizabeth didn't mind. She even accepted it when the "new Sean" became interested in Buddhism. Eventually, Sean combined Zen with spelunking, conducting meditation tours of various caves.

When Trevor wondered why he never returned to Mount Snaeffels, Sean joked, "Too many mice." Although secretly, Sean felt a twinge of fear when he recalled those dark days inside Mount Snaeffels. Some deep instinct warned him that if they had journeyed farther into the mysterious mountain, they would have discovered some terrible truth.

As for Hannah, the visions that kept her from despairing in the dark cave inspired her to do what she'd always secretly wanted to: move to Paris. She sold the institute and became a tour guide in the City of Lights. Since she was fluent in French, Croatian, and Finnish, Hannah had no trouble getting work.

Each workday, she delighted in showing tourists all the amazing things the city had to offer. Although, personally, Hannah's favorite part of Paris had to be its total lack of caves.

END.

CAVES

Hannah took three headlamps from her bag and quietly stated, "There's always another way, Sean."

Trevor put on one of the lamps and asked, "What else you got in that bag?"

Hannah recited the list of items she had memorized during many expeditions into isolated regions. "Signal flares, first aid kit, rope, a blanket, and a couple of protein bars, but those are on ration. We have no idea how long we'll be trapped."

Sean flipped open his cell phone and frantically pushed buttons. "I'm not getting a signal," Sean reported with rising anxiety.

Trevor gently explained. "We're on the top of a mountain, buried under magnetically charged rocks. Of course there's no signal."

Sean's eyes widened with fear, edging toward panic.

Too late, Trevor realized he'd just made their situation sound even worse. So he looked Sean in the eyes and said solemnly, "Sean, we're going to get out, all right? I promised your mom I'd take care of you, and I'm going to keep that promise."

Sean took a deep breath, but still felt the knot of fear twisting in his stomach. "Somehow that's not entirely comforting."

Hannah said, "C'mon. Let's find that 'other way.'"

Trevor and Sean followed the beam of Hannah's headlamp through the tunnel of rock. They soon came to a fork. Their lamps could only shine so far down each narrow passage.

Hannah said, "One of these might snake up to the surface."

Sean wondered, "Which one do we take?"

Trevor guessed, "My gut says we go right."

Since Hannah wasn't sure, Trevor took the lead. Despite the danger, he started to enjoy this subterranean hike. "Yeah, yeah, this looks like the way. I always had a nose for this stuff. Direction is, like, my sixth sense."

They squeezed past some protruding rocks and met a dead end! Trevor swept his headlamp beam over the uninterrupted wall of rock and concluded, "Turn around. Back the way we came."

Sean teased, "So what's your seventh sense?"

"From now on, you follow me," Hannah stated.

So they walked all the way back to the fork, and this time tried the left tunnel. Spiky stalagmites poked up from the floor and dagger-like stalactites jabbed down from the ceiling. Sean fought the feeling of being in the jaws of a giant monster. But Trevor chattered happily about rock formations. "You know, I've missed this—the fieldwork. I've just been cooped up in that lab all these years."

Sean shuddered. "Yeah, being caught inside a volcano is so much better."

For a few moments, they all concentrated on not tripping over any stalagmites or bumping into any of the many stalactites poking into their path.

Then Trevor saw a glittering stripe in the tunnel wall. "Crystalline striations. I wouldn't have expected to see anything like this down here . . ."

Suddenly, Hannah grabbed Trevor's shoulder and shouted, "Watch out!"

One of Trevor's feet stopped inches from the end of the path; the other hung out over a deep, dark shaft. If Trevor had taken one more step . . .

Hannah's strong hand pulled him back. "You're not studying rocks in a lab, Professor. This is life or death here."

Sean gazed down the shaft. "Do you think this leads to the center of the Earth?"

Hannah smirked.

Trevor noticed a wooden plank with the faded remains of Icelandic letters. "What's this say?"

Hannah read, "*Viourvaeri ut.* That's 'keep out.'"

"Decent advice," Sean joked.

But Hannah looked thoughtful. "No, it's good news. It might lead us into an old mine shaft and be our way out of here."

Sean's stomach churned with fear. "How, um, deep do you think it is?"

Trevor suggested, "Let me see one of the flares."

Hannah handed Trevor a flare. He dragged the tip of it across the ground and it sparked to life. Trevor said, "Sean, I'm going to drop the flare. Look at your watch and tell me how many seconds pass before it stops."

Sean lifted his wrist and tilted his headlamp so he could read the second hand on his watch. Trevor leaned against the wall behind them, and when the flare touched the wall, the rocks burst into bright white flames!

Trevor, Sean, and Hannah all dropped to the dirt.

Hannah recovered her voice first. "What was that?"

Trevor stared at the flare in his hand and then at the wall. Now he understood. "Magnesium. There must be veins running all over these walls."

Hannah said, "And magnesium is kind of flammable, right, Professor?"

Trevor nodded. "It's used in gunpowder."

Hannah sighed. "Maybe gunpowder and flares aren't such a good idea down here."

She took the flare back from Trevor and put it out. While she waited for it to cool completely, Hannah reached in her bag for a glow stick.

Trevor smiled. "Same principle—"

Hannah completed his sentence, "—with slightly less chance of blowing our heads off."

Sean nodded. Trevor dropped the stick. And as the seconds ticked off, the three travelers watched the glowing stick sinking through the empty darkness. After a few seconds, they heard a far-off clunk.

Sean said, "Three seconds. That's good, right?"

Trevor recited the formula for calculating the distance of a fall by using the speed of gravity on Earth. "Thirty-two feet per second squared, that's two-hundred feet. Your basic twenty-story high-rise."

Hannah pulled rope out of her pack. "Two hundred. No problem."

Sean objected. "Whoa, whoa, whoa—no problem for what?"

"Rappelling down in there," Hannah replied.

Panic's icy fingers closed around Sean's heart. Many years had passed since the last time he'd felt such raw, animal fear. "Rappelling down in that deep, dark hole?!"

Trevor said, "Sean, you can do this. Your father was a gifted climber. It's in your DNA."

"Well, guess what?" Sean demanded. "I didn't get that gene. And apparently neither did you. There's no way we should be rappelling down there into darkness!"

Hannah took out another heavy rope and said, "I'm going to be tethered to you both."

Sean hesitated.

If you want Sean to find another way, keep reading on page 53, Chapter: Sean's Way.

If you want Sean to face his fear, trust Hannah, Trevor, and the rope, and rappel into the dreaded darkness, keep reading on page 61, Chapter: Rappel.

SEAN'S WAY

Sean felt a strong instinct not to rappel down the shaft.

Hannah tried to reassure him. "The harness is quite secure."

"We'll both be right there with you," Trevor promised. "You'll probably love it and want to go rock climbing all the time. Your dad was a natural."

At the mention of Max, Sean finally admitted why he didn't want to go. "I think my father died down there."

Trevor did not know what to say. Sean could be right. Even with all his training, Max may have been trapped down there. And maybe, somehow, Sean could feel that.

Trevor didn't exactly believe in ESP, but he reminded himself that lots of people felt the same way about plate tectonics. All over the world, people recorded cases of telepathy or mind-to-mind communication. Most often this extrasensory perception occurred between close family members who somehow felt one another's danger or sent a long-distance warning.

Trevor looked at his nephew's troubled face and declared, "Then we'll just have to find another way."

Hannah suggested, "We can explore this passage first."

So they walked for a while through a more-or-less horizontal tunnel. For some time, the only sounds came from the travelers' footsteps and breathing. But after hours of silent hiking, Trevor heard something different. "Listen!" he exclaimed.

Hannah stopped walking. Then she heard the faint rushing sound, too.

Sean cupped his ears, trying to determine the nature of the noise. "Is it wind or water?"

Trevor cupped his ears and listened again. "I'm not sure. But either way, let's follow it!"

Once they advanced down the narrow passageway, the sound grew louder, but Sean still couldn't tell for sure what he heard. Then Sean realized the source of his confusion. "It's two sounds: wind *and* water!"

Hannah pointed ahead to a fork in the tunnel. The right branch led uphill, where the sound of water grew louder and the walls felt damp.

Sean licked his dry lips and said, "Water! Let's go there."

Trevor trotted up the left branch and reported. "I can't see anything yet. But I think I feel a breeze." He waited, then a faint breeze tickled his face again. "Yeah, that's wind."

Now Sean felt torn. A drink of water would be wonderful. But a breeze might mean freedom—fast!

If you want to follow the right branch, keep reading on page 55, Chapter: Water.

If you want to follow the left branch, keep reading on page 58, Chapter: Breeze.

WATER

Sean dropped to his knees and stuck his face in the stream before Hannah could caution, "Let's test it first!"

Fortunately for Sean, the underground spring water tasted fine, and even tested clean with a kit from Hannah's backpack.

Sean filled both hands and drank the precious liquid greedily. "Why did I ever bother with soda when water is so great?"

Trevor laughed, then listened. "It sounds like this spring picks up some speed."

"I suggest we follow it," Hannah said.

So the travelers walked beside the stream for a while. Sean took great comfort in its presence, which guaranteed he would not be thirsty for some time. Trevor told him about how the scientist in *Journey to the Center of the Earth* names a stream after their guide. Sean suggested, "Let's call this one Hannah."

Before long, Hannah-the-Stream took over the whole path and the travelers had to trudge through cold, rushing water. Having wet feet felt bad enough, but that quickly turned into wet shins, knees, and waists!

"Hang on!" Trevor said as the rising water lifted them.

But holding hands proved impossible as the rushing water pushed them down a chute into a natural water slide.

"Woo-hoo!" Sean shouted.

Trevor did not know whether to share his worries with his nephew or to just let Sean enjoy the ride while it lasted.

Hannah seemed to read the scientist's mind. She asked, "Where will this end?"

In response, Trevor's eyes only opened wider. Hannah understood that he did not know, either, and like her, Trevor feared the worst: to be drowned or dashed against rocks.

But meanwhile, Trevor flung up his arms and shouted, "Yippee!"

Hannah did the same. If these were to be their last moments of life, she agreed that they might as well have fun.

"Yippee!!!" the three shouted, then all at once they saw it— the sky!

The slide soon dumped them on the mountainside, soaked to the skin and bruised, but extremely happy to be alive.

Back in the comfort of Hannah's cozy cabin, Trevor said, "This is the most fun I've had in years! I forgot how much I love fieldwork and just being outside. I dread going back to the university."

Hannah asked, "Then why should you?"

Trevor blinked. "I'm not sure what else I could do."

Hannah laughed. "That's a silly reason for a smart man to stay miserable. You seem like a useful person. Would you like to be my assistant?"

Trevor wondered if the pretty guide could be serious.

Hannah went on, "As you've noticed, Iceland isn't exactly overrun with guides. Of course, if you'd rather return to the classroom . . ."

Trevor thought of Dean Kitzens and the gum-chewing girl. "I think the university can carry on without Professor Anderson."

Trevor turned out to be an excellent guide. Travelers enjoyed his lectures on rocks and plate tectonics. Most people who visited Iceland had an interest in such things.

Hannah always told tourists, "My assistant's name is Trevor, but you can call him Professor."

Trevor secretly liked the nickname, because it reminded him that he had moved on from a job that made him miserable to one that made him happy.

As for Sean, when he grew up, he sold the rights to his amazing adventure to a movie company. Then he invested that money by opening a super-exciting subterranean water slide at a famous amusement park in Florida. Sean added elements from Jules Verne's book to his water slide—even the battle between prehistoric beasts that one character only saw in a fever dream. The slide splashed through simulated magma, past fake geysers and bubbling pools that even smelled like sulfur. No other slide so thrillingly combined fantasy and real sensations of every possible kind.

That success led to others, for which Sean felt very grateful. But he always wondered what had happened to his father, and what they might have found if he, Trevor, and Hannah, had followed Max—and Jules Verne—into the center of the Earth.

END.

If you wonder, keep reading on page 61, Chapter: Rappel.

BREEZE

Trevor, Hannah, and Sean followed the breeze down a dark, winding passage. At each turn, they hoped to be greeted by daylight. But they soon discovered that the breeze did not come from the surface, but from a large cavern.

"We'll just have to keep exploring," Hannah said. "We can mark our trails to show where we've been."

"Good thinking," Trevor added. "Eventually we will find a way out."

But despite this brave declaration, the three travelers spent many long and dreadful days in that subterranean darkness. First they ran out of food, then water.

Knowing that the batteries in their headlamps would not last forever, they decided to limit their use to one for the leader. So Hannah wore the light as she led them through the seemingly endless maze of passageways. Trevor and Sean took turns holding her hand and each other's as they stumbled through the gloom.

Several times Sean felt so exhausted that he wanted to give up, just like the nephew in Jules Verne's book. All through the novel, the young character of Harry longs for the comforts of home, while his uncle steadfastly pursues his scientific quest. His uncle, Professor Hardwigg, is the kind of ruthless fanatic who achieves greatness because he's too focused on his goal to even consider quitting. Though far nicer than Professor Hardwigg, Trevor shared the man's fierce determination and passion for science. Hardwigg would not let his nephew give up—and neither would Trevor.

In the darkness, their other senses became more acute. Using sound, smell, taste, and touch, the travelers explored the weird, underground world. They discovered several kinds of edible mushrooms. Hannah's camp stove made insects, lizards, and the like a bit more palatable. Nothing tasted good, but they survived.

Every now and then, Trevor stopped their progress when Hannah's beam landed on a particularly amazing fossil. "I wish I had the strength to chip that out and carry it!" Then he gushed, "Just like Verne thought, these underground layers hold the whole history of life on Earth!"

Hannah bristled at the mention of Verne. But Trevor could not contain his enthusiasm for these brief glimpses of Earth's infancy written in rock.

Eventually, and amazingly, their path led them to an opening at the base of Mount Snaeffels. Sean's concerned mother immediately flew out to Iceland to see her son and brother-in-law home.

Because they did not journey all the way to the center, Trevor, Hannah, and Sean would never know that live specimens of long-"extinct" species really did exist in tunnels far deeper than those through which they journeyed.

Once he was home, the first thing Trevor did was to take the black box to the lab. If the fourth blip meant what he feared, people had to be warned! Fortunately, the data revealed that the region was prone to periodic seismic upsets.

Trevor's report on the results received rave reviews in scientific circles. A top institute offered Trevor his dream job: fully-funded research in plate tectonics. It was perfect. Trevor would be happy as long as he could work on what he wanted, where, and with whom.

Time shared in hardship had made Trevor appreciate the way Hannah's strengths complemented his own. Sometimes he got lost in science; Hannah brought him back to the here and now. Even tired, hungry, and frightened, the Icelander always kept her wits.

Trevor hoped that in time Hannah would recognize their friendship as the basis for more. So he told his future employers, "Count me in—as long as I can work from a base in Iceland!"

As for Sean, he spent every summer after that in Iceland, helping Trevor and Hannah collect data. "He gets more like Max every day," Trevor reported to Elizabeth.

"Tell me about it," Sean's mother agreed.

Sean could not explain why he felt drawn to Iceland and science after his dangerous adventure on Mount Snaeffels. Sean only knew that studying there made him feel close to his father, and that adding to humanity's understanding of our amazing planet seemed as good a way as any to spend his time.

When Sean grew up, he eventually moved permanently to Iceland, marrying a woman who raised horses. They named their three children Jules, Verne, and Max.

END.

RAPPEL

Hannah tied the ropes to the rock cliff and secured a harness on the three travelers. Trevor tried to prove that he was just as brave and capable. He said, "I'll go first to make sure it's, um, safe."

For a moment, Trevor clung to the solid ground. Then he flung himself over the edge of the cliff into the darkness. Just before his feet found the side of the shaft, Trevor felt the pure fear of Max's fall in his nightmare. Then his boots touched the rocks and he turned his attention back to the others.

Hannah dropped over the edge, instantly finding her footing.

Sean looked sick with fear, like a kid who's climbed all the way up the high diving board and now doesn't want to jump.

Hannah said, "It's okay, Sean. We are secured together. Nothing will happen."

Sean wiped his sweaty palms on his pants and reached for the rope. He realized the only thing worse than that moment would be letting the dread last any longer. Sean stepped down into the shaft and felt the harness hold his weight. His boots kicked the shaft and rocks crumbled, clattering down the cliff.

Trevor shouted, "Hey! Hey! Watch it up there!"

"I'm hanging on for my life here!" Sean replied, enormously relieved that the rocks he'd dislodged had done nothing more than annoy his uncle—and remind Sean of the frightening distance between his present location and whatever awaited them at the shaft's end.

Hannah tried to help him relax. "Just make conversation with me, Sean." The strategy worked.

As the two chatted, the scientist distracted himself from the dangerous descent by remarking on the composition of the lumpy, tan cliff against which they rappelled. Suddenly, a stone shattered under

Trevor's boot and he found himself falling backward!

He started to scream, "Oh my Goooo . . ."

Then the rope snapped tight. Trevor hung, helpless as bait, as his line twisted around Hannah's. The slender guide strained under Trevor's weight. She shouted, "Get to the wall, Trevor!"

Hannah looked down to where Trevor hung, suspended on his back, a hundred feet below them.

"I can't!" he shouted. "The walls widen down here!"

Hannah shone her headlamp down on Trevor as he kicked and wiggled in a useless attempt to pull himself closer to the wall. She stated, "Your rope's caught on mine. You're going to take us all down. I'm going to have to cut you loose!"

Trevor could not believe his ears. "Whaaaat?"

Sean could not believe the guide, either. As she flipped open her knife, he shouted, "Hannah, no!"

But Hannah sliced the rope and Trevor fell . . . a full foot-and-a-half to the ground. He landed on his most padded part with a dull thud. Trevor quickly recovered his dignity. "The, uh, bottom's right here, guys."

With a whoosh of ropes gliding through metal rings, Hannah dropped down beside him. Trevor said, "You knew that, right?"

The guide did not bother to answer. She lowered Sean gently down until his feet gratefully touched the ground.

Three bright beams of light swung around in the darkness, momentarily illuminating the sand and rock floor of a large cavern. "Where are we?" Sean asked.

Trevor's light touched on rusty rails and equally rusty mining cars. He answered, "Abandoned mine tunnel."

Hannah continued, "Old Bla'gils Mine. They shut it down sixty years ago, after the big disaster."

Sean's stomach had barely recovered from the descent. Now it churned again. "Um, how big?"

"Eighty-one dead," Hannah replied.

Trevor's lamp scanned the open area, finding more mining cars and rusty rails. Trevor shuddered. "That's pretty big."

Hannah didn't hear him. Her boots crunched briskly on the gravel as she walked on. Trevor trotted to catch up with her. He asked, "Where did you learn to speak English so well?"

"I went to boarding school in London," she replied. "The best thing my father ever did for me was to send me away."

Hannah's neutral tone did not hide the painful fact of her statement. Trevor tried to find a happier subject. "Now that he is gone, are you happy to be back home?"

"I am an Icelander," she stated. "If we Icelanders do not return, there will be no more Iceland."

Trevor glanced back. Sean walked behind them, too far away to hear his next question, "Do you ever wonder if—you know, just in theory—what if my brother and your father weren't wrong?"

Hannah's boots stopped their steady crunching. She turned to face Trevor, nearly blinding him with her headlamp. "Let me make something clear to you. I am not my father."

"I never said . . ."

Hannah interrupted, "The world he belonged to has nothing to do with me. He died in an asylum in Oslo, still raving about the center of the Earth. That, my friend, will never happen to me."

The bright blue eyes shone with fierce determination. Trevor held up his hands, as if to prove he came in peace. "I understand. I only meant . . ."

The guide had no time to discuss emotions. She reminded her employer, "I'm still on the clock, you know."

Trevor shook his head. Down here, lost in an abandoned mine that had already claimed eighty-one lives, she was calculating her paycheck? Trevor said, "Wait, you're billing me for this?"

Hannah nodded, the bright beam bouncing. "I'm billing you until I'm back, safe in my house."

The beam of Hannah's headlamp struck something shiny on the far wall. She hurried across the cavern to examine a big machine covered in buttons, knobs, and levers.

Sean and Trevor thought the ancient machine looked faintly familiar. "What is it?"

Hannah reached for a rusty lever and replied, "The old generator for the mine."

Trevor looked nervously from Hannah to the generator. He asked, "Are you sure you want to pull that?"

Hannah flipped a switch and the generator made a wheezing noise like a mummy's first gasp for breath after being awakened from the sleep of death. Hannah flipped a few more levers and . . .

Floodlights all around the travelers flickered to life. Most of the bulbs were broken, but those that worked cast an eerie, yellow glow over the cavern full of mining cars.

Sean smiled. "Wow. That's a serious generator." His grin grew wider as he added, "This is what we're looking for, right? The miners had to get their stuff out somewhere, right? So these tracks should take us out."

Trevor thought of the eighty-one people who might argue with that statement. "Hannah, did any of the miners get out?"

Hannah nodded. "Yes. One."

Trevor would have preferred a much higher number. But Sean did not care. He had already leaped into the first of two mining cars on the track near Hannah's feet. "Well, that's a start," Sean said, hastily adding, "I call front."

Trevor doubted that the rails would be safe after being abandoned for a hundred years. "Sean—get out. We'll keep walking the track."

Sean groaned. "But we've been walking forever."

"We don't even know if these things work," Trevor explained.

But just then, Hannah rode up, driving a pump car that banged into the back of the second mining car. Sean jolted forward as Hannah told Trevor, "The track ahead looks good. Get in."

Sean smiled, climbing into the first car. He would get to ride the tracks after all!

Trevor climbed into the second mining car and Hannah worked the pump car behind that. Progress at first felt slow and squeaky, but they soon gained momentum and the rock walls began to whip past them. Sean stood up and leaned out, straining to see the track ahead through the dimly lit mine.

As the three-car train rattled and roared over the tracks, Hannah's heart thumped. The wheels gathered more speed, and the tunnel turned. Sean tightened his grip on the sides of the car and bent his knees like a skateboarder bracing for a jump. His headlamp flashed over another section of rock wall, then another curve in the track. What would they see around the next bend? Sean didn't know! He screamed with a mixture of terror and joy.

They rattled past several broken mining cars. Trevor winced at the unwelcome reminder of the fate of trains that jump their tracks. He turned back to the track ahead, trying to see past Sean.

Trevor cringed as his nephew's skull skimmed the sharp boulders. "Watch it, kid. That's not safe." Despite the similarity, this was no roller-coaster ride!

"But I think I see something," Sean protested as he tried to see around the next curve. "It's—" Sean leaned out just a little farther, making his uncle even more anxious.

"Daylight?" Trevor interrupted. "Because that's all we're really interested in."

Sean sat down instantly, then stammered, not knowing how to express the awful vision. "It's, um, well—not daylight . . ." His hands clutched the sides of the car as it lurched toward a gap in the tracks. Beneath the sheer drop, the travelers saw a huge mining cavern across which broken train tracks stretched like the ribs of a long-dead behemoth. Jagged stalagmites rose in the gaps between the rails.

Sean shouted, "Hannah!"

The guide cried, "I know!"

Trevor commanded, "Pull the brakes."

Hannah knew enough about speed, momentum, and distance to make a quick, terrifying judgment. "Don't! We won't make it!"

If you agree with Trevor that they should "Pull the brakes!" go to page 66, Chapter: Brakes.

If you agree with Hannah that the best response is to pump faster, keep reading on page 123, Chapter: Jump.

BRAKES

The mining car's rusty brakes shrieked and sparked. Trevor glanced nervously from the track to the fast-approaching gap. He urged the car, "Slow down faster!"

Sean didn't bother pointing out the absurdity of his uncle's plea. He just added his own, "Come on! SLOW DOWN!"

But it was clear that Hannah was right. The gap approached faster than the cars could slow down. Trevor shouted, "Jump!"

Without hesitation, all three jumped out of the car. They hit the ground and rolled, into the walls and into one another. They looked up from the tangle of bruised limbs just in time to see their recent ride roll off the end of the track. They heard a loud crash far below and suddenly the air came to life with the frantic, outraged squeaking of a huge colony of bats!

Hannah tucked her hair inside her collar and covered her face against the swooping swarm. Not even the experienced guide could keep her cool while surrounded by so many shrill and flapping bats.

"There are no bats in Iceland!" Hannah declared.

"Tell that to the bats!" Trevor exclaimed. Actually, he had recently read an article about the discovery of five different species of the flying mammals in Hannah's homeland. Trevor didn't bother mentioning the article because he figured the bats circling Hannah's head made a better case on their own.

Trevor wondered if the unexpected presence of so many bats might be proof of Max and Verne's theories. If tunnels truly did crisscross the center of the Earth, then species like bats could shelter there in great numbers, perhaps even drawn by the warmth resulting from the seismic disturbance that the fourth blip warned of.

Iceland already offered sanctuary to huge numbers of migrating birds. Could underground tunnels be a hibernating place for giant colonies of bats? Iceland's small human population could hardly be expected to notice this subterranean invasion, which might be as recent as the fourth blip.

Sean's voice interrupted Trevor's scientific musing. "Uncle Trevor!"

"I'm here!" Trevor called. But with all the bats circling his head, Trevor could hardly see at all. He tripped over a stalagmite, and rolled down a steeply sloping tunnel branching off from the main cavern. "Oof!" he exclaimed when he hit the ground.

Sean followed the sound, but wound up walking down a tunnel beside Trevor's.

Meanwhile, Hannah had her hands full, or rather, her hair. One of the bats had tangled itself in the long, golden strands. Hannah clamped her eyes shut against the thrashing claws. She reached for her knife and gave herself a hasty haircut. The bat flapped off, trailing blond hair from its recently freed claws.

Hannah suddenly realized that she no longer heard any human sounds above the shrill shrieking. She looked around for Sean and Trevor, and saw a light disappear around a tunnel bend. Hannah ran after it, shouting, "Trevor! Sean!"

To her horror, Hannah realized the light belonged to some kind of luminous moth, not Sean or Trevor's headlamp, as she had hoped. Betrayed by sight, she followed the sound of Trevor and Sean's distant voices. But the twisting tunnels bent the sounds, tricking them all into walking farther apart, not closer. When her companions called again, Trevor and Sean sounded even farther away.

Hannah knew that sound in caves could be tricky, making far things sound near and near things sound far. She only hoped that despite this confusing obstacle, she would be able to find Trevor and Sean again.

If you want to follow Trevor's adventure, keep reading on page 69, Chapter: Trevor's Trials and Triumphs.

If you want to find out what happens to Hannah, keep reading on page 99, Chapter: Hannah Copes with Crisis.

If you want to know what happens to Sean, keep reading on page 116, Chapter: Sean's Solo Sojourn.

TREVOR'S TRIALS AND TRIUMPHS

Trevor struggled to regain his footing in the steep, dark tunnel. Still tormented by angry bats, he turned around, trying to find someplace to put his face that wasn't filled with squeaking creatures. Trevor faintly heard Hannah shouting Sean's name and his own over the horribly shrill shrieking. He walked toward the sound of her voice and called, "HAN—"

But he was interrupted by a sudden pang of pain. "OW!" he yelped. Trevor heard the crunch of breaking glass and felt a sharp pain in his head. Trevor recognized the wound from his spelunking days with Max: He had just found a low-hanging stalactite the hard way. With his headlamp crushed, Trevor's world suddenly went black! He heard Hannah's voice again and took a step toward it—but his foot had stepped once again into a gaping hole in the ground! And this time, there was no Hannah to pull him back to safety. Before Trevor could retrieve his foot from the abyss, his center of gravity had shifted and he found himself tumbling into a black void.

Trevor's arms swam through thin air. His fingers met nothing but wind. Expecting each second to be his last, Trevor shouted, "SEAN! HANNAH!" His nightmare had come to life, only instead of Max, it was Trevor who fell—and fell, and fell!

Trevor strained his ears for any sound. Even the shrieking of bats would have been welcome. The lack of sensation, except for the faint one of falling, made the experience strangely surreal. Trevor wondered, *Am I dead?* Then he shook his head. No one who was dead could feel this afraid.

Trevor distracted himself with science. "This shaft proves Verne and Max were right!"

But being right about tunnels crossing the center of the Earth did little to console someone falling through one. Trevor tried to think of possible happy outcomes from his present predicament. Would he somehow pop out of Earth's crust in China?

Trevor recalled Verne's descriptions of shafts many miles long crisscrossing the center of the Earth. *Could this be one of those shafts?* Trevor wondered. Nothing else could explain this amazing experience. *Max was right!* Trevor thought. He only hoped he'd live to prove that to the world.

Finally, a subtle sound tiptoed into the darkness; it was the drip and trickle of several underground streams. The sound grew nearer, until Trevor could even smell the dark water just before he landed in a deep, cool pool.

Trevor climbed out of the water and glimpsed lights. He began calling for his companions again. Could they have also fallen down this far? But Sean and Hannah did not answer. Trevor soon realized the lights were not the hoped-for headlamps, but the glowing bodies of bioluminescent insects.

Trevor sighed. If only he could carry the bugs' lights with him. Then he noticed something sparkling on the ground. Trevor recognized the glass-like mineral known as muscovite. He grinned as an idea came to him. Trevor pulled a roll of duct tape out of his pack and advised the glowing insects, "Don't leave home without it."

Trevor selected several large shards of muscovite and taped them together to form a crude lantern. The glowing bugs seemed to have no fear of him, so Trevor had no trouble catching a whole swarm of them to fill this clear cage.

Having a steady light source lifted his spirits. With his sight and confidence restored, Trevor searched for Hannah and Sean. Instead, he found two tunnels.

Trevor looked at each tunnel, holding his bug lantern high. Then he listened. The tunnel leading up was silent. When Trevor cupped his ear, he heard faint noises from the tunnel that led down.

If you want Trevor to go up, keep reading on page 71, Chapter: Uptunnel.

If you think Trevor should follow his ears, keep reading on page 91, Chapter: Downtunnel.

UPTUNNEL

Trevor followed the silent tunnel as it climbed slowly upward. He kept calling for Hannah and Sean, desperately listening for an answer.

The path arched, bridge-like, over another deep drop. Trevor saw no reason to turn back, until he looked down at the halfway point. Only then did Trevor realize that the center of the bridge was made of muscovite!

Trevor wondered if the fragile mineral that formed his lantern could hold his weight. The first ominous cracks under his feet answered that question. The muscovite bridge shifted and sank under his feet.

But instead of crashing into the hard, pitiless ground below, Trevor landed in something soft and squishy with a texture like moist Styrofoam. Trevor sniffed the crumbs of plant matter that had saved him from yet another fatal fall. He cautiously nibbled a piece of the familiar-smelling substance. Then he looked all around him at a forest filled with lush, weird vegetation and concluded that he had landed on a giant mushroom!

Trevor laughed. "Never been a big mushroom fan. But from now on, mushrooms are my favorite!"

Trevor filled his hungry cheeks, then stuffed his pack with mushroom snacks before scrambling down from his edible savior.

Trevor repaired his lantern with some new duct tape. "I'll replace you guys as soon as I run into a new swarm," he promised the glowing bugs. Speaking aloud only reminded Trevor of his loneliness. He had to come up with some kind of plan to find Sean and Hannah, but how?

Trevor leaned against a rock wall and tried to think. But suddenly he heard a loud crunch right behind him. Trevor's mind tried to dismiss the noise as impossible. Walls don't crunch. But after another crunching sound, Trevor saw the tip of an enormous yellow claw breaking through the solid rock!

As Trevor watched, one huge claw and then another tore through the rock wall as if it were cardboard. As the hole quickly grew, Trevor saw the monstrous arms wielding those claws and in seconds, the whole beast became visible.

The scientist gasped at what looked like a bright red, outrageously overgrown scorpion with fangs as tall as he was. The beast moved with surprising speed, moving through the hole it had just created, dragging behind it a muscular, segmented tail that looked more like a lobster's than a scorpion's.

Trevor hid behind the giant mushroom, hoping it would not be attracted to the smell of scared scientist. To his relief, the huge scorpion did not seem to notice Trevor at all. It happily dug another opening through the wall directly across from the one it had just demolished.

Well, Trevor thought. *That explains the seemingly endless supply of tunnels around here.*

As the large, lobster-like tail started to disappear through the newly created tunnel, Trevor wondered if he should follow the big beast. Terrifying as the giant scorpion looked, its presence guaranteed one good thing: Trevor would never get stuck in another dead end.

If you think he should avoid the dangerous beast, keep reading on page 73, Chapter: Avoid.

If you think Trevor should follow the giant scorpion, keep reading on page 78, Chapter: Scorpion.

AVOID

Trevor let the giant scorpion go its own way while he went his. Unfortunately, without the big beast's burrowing, Trevor did indeed keep running into dead ends.

Each time, Trevor's spirits sank. "Not again!" Was all his effort of walking wasted?

Trevor's mood became as black as the tunnels through which he wandered. The frustrated scientist thought he would go crazy. Trevor screamed, "Argh! NOT AGAIN!"

Expecting no more reply than the usual echo, Trevor nearly dropped his makeshift lantern when he heard Hannah's voice.

"Trevor?" Hannah called.

"Uncle Trevor!" Sean shouted.

Trevor raised his lantern and shouted again. "Sean! Hannah!"

"We're here!" Hannah shouted back. Although where exactly "here" was took quite some time to determine in the maze of tunnels.

By the time the three travelers were reunited, their voices had gone completely hoarse.

Trevor hugged his nephew until the teenager begged for mercy. "I'm sorry," Trevor said, adding in a hoarse voice choked with emotion, "it's just that I thought I'd lost you forever."

Then Sean laughed. "Hey, I thought I'd lost me, too."

Hannah wiped sweat off the back of her neck. "We thought we'd lost you for sure when we fell such a long way."

Trevor nodded. "Apparently Verne was right about the center of the Earth being crisscrossed with long tunnels." Trevor added, "In any case, at least we're all together. Now we just have to find a way out of here before we boil like lobsters in a pot." Trevor had no time to explain plate tectonics to his companions. But the fourth blip indicated dangerous activity beneath the Earth's crust, which was responsible for the rising temperatures that would soon reach deadly levels.

Heavy rocks tumbled to the floor near them. Hannah jumped and said, "I think we have another problem."

Trevor recognized the yellow claws tearing through the rocks. "Giant burrowing scorpion," he remarked casually. He tried to reassure Sean, "Probably not as dangerous to us as it looks."

Sean seemed skeptical. "Yeah, right. What about those guys?"

Just beyond the circle of light cast by Trevor's lantern and the others' headlamps, Trevor glimpsed an alarming array of eyes. The scientist had no way of knowing what kind of creatures surrounded them, staring with curiosity and probably hunger. He swallowed hard. "I . . . guess calling to each other for so long might have made our neighbors curious."

Sean tilted his head back until his headlamp shone on the scorpion's six-foot fangs. Sean shuddered.

He looked at his uncle, whose sweat-smeared face wore that scientist-hatching-a-theory expression. Sean asked, "What?"

Trevor replied, "Nothing grows that big in a short time. If this isn't the first seismic disaster in this region, maybe these animals have some way of surviving."

Sean seized on this scrap of hope.

Hannah wondered, "What are you suggesting?"

"I say we follow the scorpion," Trevor suggested.

Despite the beast's terrifying appearance, Hannah felt too tired and overheated to argue.

Besides, the eyes at the edge of the light seemed to be moving nearer. She agreed, "Let's go!"

Trevor, Hannah, and Sean followed the scorpion through old tunnels and the new ones it carved with its giant, yellow claws. The travelers barely noticed the heat slowly easing. They were too busy keeping up with their frightening guide.

The scorpion stopped for nothing, except to eat. When it encountered smaller creatures, the beast either seized them with its claws or clubbed them with its heavy tail.

Fortunately for the travelers, the scorpion tossed away the not-

so-meaty parts, on which Trevor, Hannah, and Sean feasted.

"I wish we had time for the camp stove," Hannah remarked. "Some of this wouldn't be bad if we cooked it."

Trevor nodded. "I bet our friend here wouldn't be bad himself with a hot tub full of melted butter."

He turned to Sean, hoping his nephew would join in the joke. But the young man seemed to be sleeping on his feet. Trevor nudged him and said, "I know it's hard, Sean. But we have to keep up."

Sean's eyes opened. "Huh? Wha . . . ?"

Trevor patted Sean's shoulder. Then he asked Hannah, "Check the temperature, please. I'm sure it's getting cooler."

The thermometer confirmed what they all already felt. "It's ten degrees cooler than when we started following our friend."

Trevor grinned. "We may get out of here yet!"

Indeed, the giant scorpion led the travelers safely away from the seismic disturbance predicted by Max's sensor. They followed the creature for six weeks, living on the scraps of its meals—and scraps of hope. The longer they spent in the dark, the more Sean despaired of ever seeing sunlight again.

Then one day, Trevor asked, "Do you smell something?"

Hannah sniffed the air. It smelled fresh, and she could almost detect the scent of flowers!

"Look!" Sean shouted.

The others now saw the light, too. The glow did not match any of their subterranean light sources. It was, Sean realized with a fluttering heart, daylight!

The scorpion had no interest in a vent leading to the surface, so they parted company.

"I'm going to miss you, you big lug," Trevor told its departing tail. Then he turned to Sean and Hannah and whispered, "Not really."

Sean laughed. In fact he could barely stop laughing the whole time they climbed up to the surface. "What's so funny?" Hannah finally asked.

Sean shook his head. "I'm just so *happy*!"

When they stepped out of the mountain and stood with the open sky over their heads, Hannah burst out laughing, too. They danced in silly circles until they fell down dizzy.

Hannah examined their surroundings: She saw snowy mountain peaks, and beyond a jagged coastline, there was a pristine ocean. But where did all the pine trees come from? She gasped, "We're not in Iceland anymore!"

Trevor agreed. "We must have come up through a different volcano."

Sean asked, "You mean you don't know where we are?"

Hannah suggested, "If we follow the coastline, we're likely to come to a town eventually."

"Great, more walking," Sean said sarcastically.

But the travelers did not have to walk far. Shortly after they reached the coast, Trevor spotted a ship. The three travelers waved excitedly. Passengers on the ship waved back in a friendly way. Then someone must have looked at the lonely, ragged figures through a telescopic lens, because the ship steered closer to where Trevor, Sean, and Hannah stood and dispatched a dinghy.

The sailor piloting the boat asked, "How'd you get here?"

Trevor looked at Sean and Hannah and smiled. "That's a long story." Then he noticed the name stenciled on the boat. Trevor gasped, "*Alaska Angel*. We're in Alaska?!"

The ship gladly took them onboard and dropped them off at their next port, where Sean and Trevor caught a plane back to the lower forty-eight. Hannah decided to stay for a few days. She had never been to the United States, and Alaska reminded her of her home in Iceland.

Elizabeth's joy at seeing her long-lost son and brother-in-law might only have been exceeded by Sean's joy at being "out from under." He didn't even mind that his summer vacation was nearly over. Starting at a new school in a new country would be a piece of cake compared to what he'd just been through.

Trevor thought about trying to mount a proper expedition. But he knew that would be even more difficult than getting funding for Max's lab, since no one believed their amazing adventure. And even if they could, Trevor did not want to travel to the center of the Earth. After that terrifying experience, he preferred to stay where scorpions are small enough to squish with a shoe.

Trevor stayed at his university job just long enough to finish his contract. Then he moved to Canada to be near Sean and Elizabeth. There, Trevor worked for various oil and natural gas companies, until he fell in with a group of scientists studying Bigfoot. Since Trevor was used to no one believing him, he fit right in with these "myth chasers." Though they never did find hard evidence of Bigfoot, Trevor made several significant discoveries during his travels with the group, including a new species of butterfly he named *Maximum Beauty*.

As for Hannah, she fell in love with Alaska, which had many of Iceland's charms, but with more excitement. As a mountain guide in Alaska, Hannah met many more interesting people. And, as long as they wanted to travel on—not inside—a mountain, Hannah was happy.

END.

SCORPION

The scorpion's tunnels took Trevor into the heart of a primitive world under a glowing stone ceiling. Trevor marveled at the plant and animal life. It was a scientist's dream come true, except that he kept having the frightening feeling that he was being followed.

Trevor did a quick fake-out, pretending to start walking again, but instantly turning around.

Trevor blinked. Did he just see that wall move? Trevor shook his head. *Walls don't move.* But when he looked more closely, it expanded and contracted in a familiar rhythm. It was breathing!

Then suddenly, the wall uncurled, revealing a gorilla-like beast covered in rocky scales. The ten-foot-tall creature opened its huge mouth and roared, thumping its muscular chest like a giant drum!

Every hair on the back of Trevor's neck stood at attention. Then, to his horror, other parts of the tunnel wall sprang to life as the rest of a troop of Rockillas joined their leader.

Trevor knew something of primate behavior. If these weird, rocky apes resembled surface gorillas in more ways than just appearance, then the leader's chest thump was a challenge. Trevor tried to recall gorilla etiquette. What would be the proper response if you wanted to make friends and not get clobbered?

If you think Trevor should thump his chest in reply, keep reading on page 79, Chapter: Thump.

If you think Trevor should run, keep reading on page 82, Chapter: Run.

If you think Trevor should search his pack for something to dazzle the apes, keep reading on page 85, Chapter: Dazzle.

THUMP

Trevor puffed up his chest and pounded on it with his fists. He roared as loud as he could.

The resulting display might have impressed other humans, and possibly even a timid gorilla. But to these ten-foot, underground, rocky-scaled apes, Trevor appeared a pathetic weakling.

Their leader stepped toward Trevor, took a deep breath, and roared so loudly he nearly knocked Trevor down with the heat, stink, and sheer force of his breath. When the leader thumped his mighty chest, it sounded like thunder echoing off the tunnel walls.

With one swipe of his mighty arm, the leader tossed Trevor aside.

"No!" he yelled, but Trevor's words went unheeded.

The scientist flew through the air and landed with a thump against the rock wall. Trevor groaned in pain as his fingers found the bloody spot on the back of his head. Trevor looked up at the creatures. Who were they? And, for that matter, who was he? Trevor seemed to have lost his memory when the creature threw him against the wall.

The leader thumped his chest, but in a quiet, time-to-break-up-the-meeting sort of way. Trevor's dazed eyes looked deep into the beast's. Trevor saw strength and courage there.

The leader started walking away. The rest of the troop followed, roughly arranged according to their status within the group.

Trevor looked around the dark tunnel at the backs of the retreating creatures, whom Trevor began referring to as Rockillas. He did not want to be alone, so he followed them.

The Rockillas could not understand the seismic disturbance indicated by the fourth blip, but as the temperature rose, they sought the safety of a place protected by ultra-thick walls from seismic events like rising magma. Trevor felt more comfortable as soon as they reached a cool, green, underground jungle. But even though his headache passed, his memory did not return.

Not knowing what else he could or should be doing, Trevor imitated the Rockillas. He ate what they ate, slept when they slept, and became accepted as an underling in the troop.

Sometimes Trevor's troop would meet another in the maze of subterranean tunnels. Chests would be thumped and occasionally someone would get hurt.

But thanks to his low status, Trevor never made it to the front lines in these territorial wars. As such a strange and puny specimen, Trevor, of course, did not have a mate. But he never lacked for companions among the friendly troop. He lived out the rest of his natural life as an underground ape, unaware of anything else, or the people who missed him.

Hannah and Sean literally bumped into each other in the dark beneath Mount Snaeffels. Sean had seen another frightening flock of swarming bats and ran blindly down the next tunnel he could find—right into Hannah!

"Where's Trevor?" they both asked at once.

While searching for him, they found a vent leading up to the surface of Mount Snaeffels.

Hannah made many attempts to retrieve her missing employer. But no trace of Trevor was ever found. For the rest of their lives, one question haunted both survivors: What happened to Trevor? Hannah and Sean would never know. And strangely enough, neither would he.

Sean felt drawn to follow in Trevor and Max's footsteps. But because he wasn't a "born scientist," Sean found a way to make plate tectonics fun for everyone. With help from Hannah, Sean organized plate tectonics tours of Iceland's amazing geology.

For many years, Sean secretly hoped that they would somehow find Trevor. Though this never happened, Sean and Hannah did help awaken many people to the fascinating field of plate tectonics, and to an appreciation of Iceland's unique beauty.

Every summer, Elizabeth visited her son. Weather permitting, Sean and Hannah would take her to Mount Snaeffels on the first of July.

Elizabeth said, "Your father and uncle would be very proud of you."

Sean nodded. "I always feel close to Dad and Trevor up here, especially on the kalends."

Hannah habitually scoffed at such Vernian nonsense. But she, too, glanced at the crater, secretly hoping the long-lost travelers would emerge from that enigmatic mountain.

END.

RUN

Trevor dug his toes into the ground, then pushed off like a power sprinter. As vegetarians, not predators, the gorilla-like creatures did not have the reflexes to give chase. But they watched with interest as Trevor's running attracted the attention of a pack of raptor-like creatures whose transparent skin revealed their glowing, green skeletons and brightly-colored internal organs.

Trevor had never imagined anything as terrifying as these Celloraptors! He wanted to stay well clear of their sharp claws and jagged teeth. But, as in some sort of dreadful nightmare, wherever he went, another pack member popped up.

The Celloraptors moved quickly and tirelessly in pursuit of their peculiar prey. Sweat poured down Trevor's face as he desperately fled the predators. But the farther he ran, the lower the external temperature seemed to be. The fourth blip predicted seismic disaster, including rising magma bringing deadly heat. Yet he felt a slight shiver across his brow where his sweat cooled.

Trevor's legs shook with the constant effort to dodge the freakish beasts. The Celloraptors reminded him of the clear plastic Visible Man model he and Max put together as boys. *What would Max do?* Trevor wondered.

A Celloraptor lunged for him and Trevor knew: Max would run! So Trevor ran his wobbly legs off. Puzzled and relieved, Trevor felt the cool rocks of the nearest wall. *What happened to the seismic catastrophe?* he thought. *I should've been roasted by now.*

Trevor wondered if the Celloraptors had chased him away from the seismic event. Had his hunters really been his saviors? Trevor heard the clatter of claws nearby. They had found him again!

The ground shook. Trevor and the Celloraptors all looked toward a tunnel through which a herd of rhinoceros-like creatures ran. The Celloraptors took off after the herd, in pursuit of dinner.

Trevor collapsed against the wall, weak with exhaustion and relief. Finally, he had a chance to catch his breath and think. Apparently the underground was as intensely crisscrossed with tunnels as Verne thought, and the pack had chased Trevor away from the big heat wave. Trevor fervently hoped that Sean and Hannah had also somehow avoided the expected eruption.

The other two travelers had encountered an underground spring that eventually led them to the surface. Sean and Hannah assisted a rescue crew in their search for Trevor, and one day, he miraculously emerged on his own through a vent in Mount Snaeffels's crater. Sweat-streaked, with torn clothes and a weary expression after weeks of climbing, Trevor looked like the survivor of a shipwreck. He blinked like a mole in the bright sunlight.

When the three were reunited, Sean rushed into his uncle's arms. Trevor wept openly. "You're alive!" Then he saw Hannah and added, "You're both alive!"

Hannah's blue eyes also filled with tears. "It's good to see you, too, Professor."

Trevor recovered from his arduous adventure with nothing worse to show for his terrifying time alone in the tunnels than some scars on his knees and elbows from repeated scraping on rocks. But that didn't interfere with his new career.

Trevor decided to follow in Jules Verne's footsteps and become a science fiction writer. Under the name Anderson Maxwell, Trevor presented Max's theories on plate tectonics to curious young minds. If the clear-skinned raptors made famous in his first book were based on truth, well, that remained Trevor's secret.

Sean only told his closest friends about his uncle's subterranean adventure, because he did not want people to think he was crazy. Hannah, on the other hand, embraced Verne, whom she had formerly despised. Now that she knew from her own experience that *Vernian* did not mean *fool*, Hannah started a successful business showing tourists "Jules Verne's Iceland."

The tour's highlights included a stroll through Reykjavík and a dip in a natural hot tub, the same kind of volcanic pool in which Iceland's first settlers soaked sore muscles, cooked food, and did their laundry.

And, of course, they visited Mount Snaeffels.

Though she did not dare risk leading travelers inside the mountain, for many, the guide's recollections of her friend Trevor's amazing journey to the center of the Earth was the best part of the tour.

END.

DAZZLE

Trevor dug through his pack, swiftly searching for something that would impress an ape. A bright, round object caught his eye. Like his brother, Trevor had always loved yo-yos. Maybe these rocky apes would like yo-yos, too. Trevor slipped the string over his finger and tossed the yo-yo out and back several times fast.

The animals hooted in excitement, looking to Trevor like the audience at a magic show when it oohs and aahs over some impossible feat. "Wait until you see me 'walk the dog,'" Trevor announced.

The gorilla-like animals tapped their foreheads in awed disbelief. Clearly this small, strange, two-legged animal knew vastly more than they, for how else could he control the bright, flying thing?

The creatures bowed to acknowledge their new leader. Trevor realized that this could have its advantages. Using sign language, Trevor managed to make the creatures, which he came to name Rockillas, understand that he needed to find his companions.

Tracking the unusual smell of human beings did not pose a problem for the underground apes. Trevor struggled to keep up with the Rockillas as they quickly sniffed through the maze of tunnels.

Within the hour, Trevor caught a glimpse of headlamps up ahead. "Sean! Hannah!"

The two turned and saw Trevor surrounded by giant, gray apes covered in rocky scales. Hannah opened her mouth to scream, but Trevor held up his hand and said, "It's okay! This is my posse."

Sean stared at his uncle in amazement.

"You'll get used to it—if we live that long," Trevor said, wiping sweat off his brow. "We need to get out of this heat!" If the fourth blip meant what Trevor feared, Mount Snaeffels was due for disaster. The sweltering heat, growing worse by the minute, confirmed his concerns. On their trip to cool ground, Sean and Hannah explained to Trevor that they had taken a fall through a chasm similar to the one

Trevor had fallen down. Luckily, though, they had not been alone as Trevor had been.

Between sign language and charades, Trevor told his troop about the imminent danger of the rising heat. They knew something had changed to make their habitat so hot. The Rockillas also knew a path to "the cold place."

The journey took a very long time, but several large lagoons along the way provided provisions, plus a chance to cool off in a pool. Many dangerous and exhausting miles later, the temperatures finally started to drop.

"We must be far enough away from the disturbance," Trevor said. But where were they?

Trevor's troop understood that he and the other small two-legs came from above the surface. But they did not want their new leader to leave. They wanted Trevor to teach them all his clever tricks. Unlike his Tectonics 101 students, the Rockillas wanted to learn! Trevor felt torn.

If you think Trevor should stay with the Rockillas, keep reading on page 87, Chapter: Ruler of the Rockillas.

If you think Trevor should search for a vent to the surface with Hannah and Sean, keep reading on page 89, Chapter: Normal Life.

RULER OF THE ROCKILLAS

Sean could not believe Trevor decided to stay underground, but the scientist did not regret his unconventional choice. Trevor became an underground Tarzan, gradually teaching the Rockillas language, art, and the other benefits of human culture.

He delighted the troop's children by making yo-yos, Frisbees, and other toys. Trevor taught them games and songs. Thanks to his healthy, natural lifestyle, Trevor lived long enough to see those children grow up to pass along his lessons.

In time, Trevor came to believe that his efforts might in some small way preserve humanity should some environmental disaster wipe out the world above. Besides, Trevor had to admit that being the smartest guy in the room had its perks. On the surface he had been a harried professor begging for funding. Inside the Earth, Trevor became the leader of a civilization.

Occasionally, the one-time professor would dimly recall the rival from his former life, Kitzens. Then he would think with great satisfaction, *Leader of an underground paradise beats Dean any day!*

Hannah found herself teaching, too. During their journey back to the surface, she taught Sean survival skills and the Icelandic songs and stories of her childhood. After their return to civilization, Hannah became a traveling teacher, touring elementary schools all over the country, preserving and spreading Icelandic culture.

When Sean grew up, he followed his father and uncle into plate tectonics. While he worked on his master's degree, Sean established an online network of student scientists all over the world.

Once all the data had been collected from seismic sensors all over the planet, "proper" scientists finally acknowledged the danger of these seismic shifts. Thanks to the rise in seismic awareness, several cities evacuated before disasters, saving countless lives. Sean only wished somehow Trevor could know that their journey to the center of the Earth was not wasted.

END.

NORMAL LIFE

The loyal Rockillas reluctantly escorted their leader and his companions to the edge of their territory. They even supplied them with several packages of fruit, insects, and lizards to eat.

Since Hannah cautiously kept them on low rations, the food lasted longer than their trek to the surface through a volcanic vent. Indeed, less than a day after saying good-bye to his troop, Trevor found himself blinking in the sunlight over Mount Snaeffels.

"Wow! I'm glad that's over!" Sean exclaimed.

Hannah agreed. "I'll stick to the outside of mountains from now on."

They turned to Trevor, who did not know what to say. Finally he admitted, "I miss those darn Rockillas."

Sean laughed. But Hannah understood. Though primitive, the Rockillas had a gentleness and grandeur of spirit most often found in the wild in species like their surface-dwelling cousins, the gorillas.

Hannah suggested, "Maybe you should get a job working with apes."

Trevor dismissed this. "No. I have to . . ." He thought of Dean Kitzens and his voice trailed off.

Hannah grinned. "Maybe you should just follow your heart."

"What kind of job could I get working with apes?" Trevor scoffed.

"I don't know yet," Hannah said. "But I'm going to find out for myself." Then she explained, "I liked them, too. I'm going to see if I can work at a game preserve or an animal park."

Trevor imagined himself tending great apes in a wild, natural setting. He smiled and said, "Sounds like a plan. When do we start?"

Hannah held out her hand. "As soon as you pay for this expedition, Professor. I'll need money for new equipment, travel expenses, and . . ." She looked down at her grubby self. ". . . a lot of bubble bath."

Sean felt no urge to work with apes, but he did go into plate tectonics. Using surveillance cameras mounted on robots, he eventually proved Max and Verne right about the amazing abundance of life inside the center of the Earth, and gained worldwide recognition.

END.

DOWNTUNNEL

Trevor followed the tunnel down into the warm darkness. He looked around for Sean and Hannah. But it seemed he had descended into a world that only included rocks and heat.

Damp hair and clothes stuck to his sweaty skin. Every muscle cried for rest and refreshment. But instead, Trevor kept trekking down the seemingly endless tunnel.

Trevor's thighs shook with fatigue. But no extreme discomfort of his body could compare to the steady ache of doubt weighing on Trevor's mind.

What if all this effort was taking him in the wrong direction? Should he turn back or keep going down?

If you think Trevor should go farther down into the center of the Earth, keep reading on page 92, Chapter: Down, Down, Down.

If you think Trevor should turn back, keep reading on page 95, Chapter: Turn Back.

DOWN, DOWN, DOWN

The deeper Trevor descended, the more lonely and frightened he felt. Verne and Max were right: There was a way into the center of the Earth through Mount Snaeffels. But what good was being right down here, alone in the dark?

In this seemingly bottomless pit, Trevor confronted his darkest demons. How had it come to this? What kind of fool drags his nephew into such danger? Why couldn't he let go of his brother and his scientific ambitions?

Trevor imagined the horrible ordeal Elizabeth would endure if he and Sean disappeared like Max. Hadn't his sister-in-law suffered enough already?

"What was I thinking?" Trevor asked the pitiless rocks. Then he shouted in anguish and remorse, "How could I be such a FOOL?!"

Trevor slumped, exhausted, and too disgusted with himself to go on. And then, as if the rocks could somehow absolve him, Trevor shouted at the top of his lungs, "I'M SORRY! I'M SO SORRY!"

"For what?" Hannah's voice asked, sounding as if the guide stood only a few feet away. Trevor thought he'd lost his mind. He shouted, "Hannah?"

"Yes! We're both here!"

Trevor heard their voices, but he could not see his companions. His heart leaped with joy as he wondered, "Where is 'here'?"

Sean's laughter carried across what turned out to be quite a long distance of winding tunnels.

"This must be a 'whispering arch,' like in Verne's book," Trevor remarked.

Sean reminded his uncle that he still hadn't read *Journey to the Center of the Earth*.

Trevor explained, "It's a trick of sound that sometimes happens in big cathedrals, giant halls, and . . . certain caves. It must have something to do with the curvature of the cave's ceiling. But basically, it carries the sound farther than it would normally travel."

Sean felt strange. His uncle sounded near enough to touch, but his headlamp showed no sign of him.

Hannah said, "'Whispering arch' or whatever, just keep talking."

"I know," Trevor said. "How about we find each other and a way out of here!"

Sean liked that idea. And, in fact, shortly after their happy reunion, he spotted a vent that luckily led back up to the surface. But where the vent led them took Trevor by complete surprise. Before long, their feet and ankles were wet with muddy liquid.

Sean gagged. "What's that smell?"

Trevor looked at the tunnel's concrete walls—way too smooth to be natural rock.

Hannah sniffed and remarked, "I think we're in a sewer!"

Trevor saw a Day-Glo sign beside a small pipe up ahead.

Sean caught up to him and read, "NYC sewer—as in New York City?"

Trevor shook his head. "Impossible!"

Hannah tapped Trevor's shoulder. "We're not alone, Professor."

Trevor turned just in time to see a giant alligator rushing straight toward them!

Sean screamed!

Hannah shouted, "Run!"

The three took off down the tunnel with the alligator splashing angrily behind them.

Sean gasped, "What do we do?"

"Keep running!" Hannah advised.

Trevor looked back and saw the alligator open its huge jaws. Motivated by its impressive array of teeth, Trevor ran faster.

Soon, the long-legged humans outdistanced the reptile. The travelers bent over to catch their breath.

They came to a ladder leading up to the street. When Trevor cautiously lifted the heavy manhole cover, his ears instantly rang with the full symphony of Midtown traffic. He ducked back down to report, "We're on Fifth Avenue, not far from the Empire State Building."

Hannah had as much trouble as Trevor accepting the impossible. "But how . . . ?"

Sean exclaimed. "Who cares? We're here! We can go home!"

The busy New Yorkers and tourists paid no attention to the dazed and dirty travelers. They had seen it all, it seemed. Trevor's credit card bought them a hotel suite and the bubble bath of Hannah's dreams. Sean immediately called his mother and ordered enough pizza for twenty people.

Elizabeth could not stay angry at Sean and Trevor for "falling off the edge of the Earth" for several days.

"Actually, 'into the Earth,'" Sean corrected his mother. "But we're fine now. And I'll be home in time to help you unpack."

After his ordeal in the dark mountain, Sean did not resent his upcoming move to Canada quite so much. "As long as I'm above ground," he told Trevor, "I'm happy."

Hannah and Trevor could not wait to go back inside Mount Snaeffels. Having discovered that they worked well together, Hannah helped Trevor raise money for a proper scientific expedition. This took many years but proved well worth the effort, yielding many important discoveries. Trevor retired only after accomplishing many of the lofty goals he and Max had dreamed up in their childhood. And it never would have worked out so well if Trevor had not dared to journey to the center of the Earth.

END.

TURN BACK

Trevor trudged back up the way he came. With each step, he felt more tired and hungry. Trevor tried to keep moving, but the oppressive heat finally forced him to his knees. Trevor slumped against the rock wall. He thought, *Can't quit! Must keep trying.*

Without realizing he had fallen asleep, Trevor dreamed of walking through the same dark, endless tunnels.

"Trevor?" Hannah's voice intruded on his dull dream.

"UNCLE TREVOR!" Sean shouted.

"Huh? Wha . . . ?" For a moment, Trevor believed he was in his messy apartment and once again late for work.

Then Hannah's headlamp beam shone on his face and Trevor remembered their situation. "How did you . . ." he began.

But Hannah shook her head. She did not want Trevor to move until she knew his condition. She knelt behind him and gently lifted one eyelid to watch Trevor's pupil contract in the light. "Are you okay?"

Trevor nodded, but still seemed confused.

Hannah asked, "Did you take a long fall to get here?"

Trevor nodded again. "Thought I was doomed to splat."

Sean chimed in, "Except for the are-we-gonna-splat part, whatta ride, huh?"

Trevor smiled wanly. "The heat . . ." he began, until Hannah shushed him again. "We found what looks like a way to the surface. We were just going to start climbing when Sean saw the faint glow."

Trevor looked at his bug lantern. His bioluminescent buddies still glowed dully, but the bugs probably needed food. Trevor lifted the lantern's lid, let them escape, and whispered, "Thank you!"

Sean shook his head. "Talking to bugs, what's next?"

Trevor accepted a few chunks of cooked lizard from Hannah.

"Mmm. Thank you! That's . . . surprisingly good."

Hannah had been using her survival skills to make a fire and roast what animals she could. She chuckled. "I'll tell the chef."

Trevor felt his strength returning with each bite. Sean felt relieved to hear his uncle sounding like his old self. "What's next?" Trevor asked. "I guess we start climbing, huh?"

Hannah looked thoughtful. "Our packs are stuffed with food already."

Trevor understood. "I ran out of giant mushroom snacks."

Sean suggested, "Then I guess we do some fast grocery shopping before we start?" Now that he had mastered the art of lizard catching, Sean wanted to show off for his uncle.

He and Hannah led Trevor to their nearby fishing hole. Actually, the clear underground pool teemed not with fish, but with pale, blind, and tasty lizards. Sean skillfully grabbed the reptiles and handed them to Hannah. With the speedy efficiency of an expert fisherman, the guide cleaned the catch, then sprinkled the meat with salt before briefly cooking the lizards on her camp stove. Then she crammed every corner of Trevor's pack with the nutritious reptiles.

Trevor asked, "So where is this possible route to the surface?"

Just past the lizard pond, Hannah showed Trevor a shaft about three feet wide. Its steep sides seemed to climb up without end. Trevor tried to see the top, but he could not. Still, a far-off light definitely came from above.

Trevor shrugged. "This won't be an easy climb. But at least it should get us away from the heat."

Hannah looked concerned. "Are you ready?"

Trevor did not even want to think of how tired he felt. Instead, he smiled and said, "Ready as I'll ever be."

Hannah took the harness out of her pack. "We'll be linked, in case anyone . . ." her voice trailed off.

Trevor nodded.

Sean said, "Now that we've found Trevor, I'm sure everything's going to be fine."

But the miracle of finding one another in the dark underground maze could not guarantee success. Climbing up the shaft proved incredibly slow and painful. Every inch of progress was paid for in sweat and sore muscles.

For Sean, the worst part became wondering if all this effort would be wasted. Did the shaft even reach the surface?

And then they came to a few places where the distance between the walls shrank so much that they were nearly impassible. Hannah had to push her pack through first, then squeeze through behind it.

Sean grew more and more nervous. What if the shaft became even narrower up above?

Trevor shouted encouragement from below. "You can do it! Just keep on moving!"

Hannah's words helped even more. "It's okay, Sean. The shaft gets wider soon."

Sean shoved his pack into Hannah's hands. Then he took a deep breath and squeezed through the narrow passage.

Each time the shaft narrowed, Sean felt the same dread. What if he got stuck? But luckily, they all grew thinner as they ascended, making it easier to squeeze through tight spaces. Hannah strictly rationed the cooked lizards, and even so, their supply ran out long before the shaft did.

Guts growling, the travelers just kept climbing. Finally, the light at the top became brighter.

"Can you see anything?" Trevor called.

Hannah stared at the distant patch of light. Was it really sky? Could their goal at last be in sight?

Then a graceful shape flitted across the light. Hannah gasped. "A bird!" She could hardly believe her eyes. Then she saw another!

Despite their thirst, hunger, and the worst case of muscle burn ever, the three travelers quickly climbed up the rest of the shaft. The joy they felt on emerging from Mount Snaeffels defied description.

Trevor gazed adoringly at the open sky and declared, "That is the last time I ever go inside a mountain. In fact, I think I'll spend the rest of my life outside."

Sean laughed. "Yeah, right. Like you'd ever give up your lab and your blips."

To Sean's surprise, Trevor kept his word. Once they returned to civilization, the former scientist quit his university job to become a mail carrier. Each day, Trevor walked for hours through the fresh air. Most people on his route looked forward to seeing him. After all, mail carriers often bring good news (although, of course, there were bills, too). After his time alone in the dark, Trevor found he enjoyed this frequent friendly contact.

Though Trevor's body recovered completely from their underground adventure, his scientific curiosity did not survive the trip. Trevor no longer cared about the mysterious movements going on inside the center of the Earth. He just wanted a steady job, out and about under the open sky.

Sean discovered that he liked catching his own food and became a serious fisherman. Apparently he inherited Max's talent for fly tying, for which passionate trout fishermen paid excellent prices.

During a fishing trip to Iceland, Sean and Hannah collaborated on a book describing the country's best fishing spots. This led to other books and articles that allowed Sean to fish all over the world.

Trevor eventually amassed an amazing collection of postcards from his nephew, all of which began, "Just dropping you a line . . ."

END.

HANNAH COPES WITH CRISIS

The dark tunnel Hannah had walked into was not free of bats. When one of the flying creatures flew straight at her face, she stepped sideways without looking. Her foot touched the edge of an abyss. Hannah teetered on the brink, pinwheeling her arms frantically, and then she tumbled down a dark shaft. She was falling and falling—it seemed like the fall would never end. In fact, Hannah's headlamp showed steep, dark walls that went on forever. She reached for her anchor. But the smooth shaft offered no promising places for its sharp prongs to catch. Hannah hated to admit it, but perhaps Jules Verne, her father, and her employer's brother might have been right. For what else could this endless shaft be but one of the tunnels Verne proposed?

Hannah didn't know what she would find if she ever stopped falling. She hoped it would not be a rock floor, spiky with stalagmites. Yet the realistic guide knew this was a strong possibility. As a distant light grew nearer, Hannah murmured the simple phrase that always got her through tough climbs: Please give me strength!

Hannah's headlamp swept over rippling, blue water just before she splashed into a subterranean lagoon. The guide scrambled on top of a floating log and paddled to shore. All around the lagoon, an amazing abundance of life flourished. Ferns as tall as trees stretched toward the luminous, sky-like rock ceiling. Every thicket seemed alive with the constant movement of busy birds, insects, and weird reptiles.

Two things were uppermost on the guide's mind: finding her companions and surviving in this dangerous environment. Since Verne was right about life inside Earth, Hannah worried she would encounter the giant, prehistoric beasts he described.

If you think Hannah should establish a means of survival first, then look for her companions, keep reading on page 101, Chapter: Survive.

If you think Hannah should search for Trevor and Sean first, keep reading on page 106, Chapter: Rescue.

SURVIVE

Hannah hoped the big beasts had just been the "fiction" part of Mr. Verne's science fiction story. But she soon found a huge rib cage almost as tall as she was! Hannah did *not* want to see those bones dressed with hungry flesh. More importantly, she wanted to make sure that such a beast did not see her.

Hannah looked at the ribs again. Covered with ferns, the cage might make a shelter. From this hiding place, Hannah could secretly observe the weird wildlife.

Using her knife to hack down some ferns, Hannah quickly camouflaged the cage. Soon she stood inside her crude shelter, peeking out from the gaps between spiky green leaves.

Everywhere Hannah looked, creatures flew, hopped, lumbered, and leaped. They ranged from tiny insects to something so big Hannah mistook it for a distant mountain streaked with lava, until it moved. When this red behemoth reared up, she saw its green belly and huge yellow claws. But the truly heart-stopping feature had to be its fangs. Hannah tried to judge the distance between her and the monster, whose shape suggested a scorpion-lobster mix on steroids. As she watched, this huge scorpion burrowed into a rock wall, tearing through the rocks as easily as a mole tunneling through a flower bed.

The ground shook! A herd of huge, maroon beasts lumbered closer to the lagoon. These Ceratopses looked like triceratops, but with one horn instead of three.

Hannah's rational mind kept insisting that dinosaurs were extinct. But these living reptiles certainly looked the part. Hannah saw a beast that looked like a raptor, but whose clear skin revealed glowing green bones and bright innards. Anything with claws and teeth that long and sharp couldn't be cuddly. Hannah muttered softly, "Great: disgusting *and* deadly!"

She held her breath as the Celloraptor advanced on the herd. Suddenly, a bright light dazzled the predator and Hannah, as the lead Ceratops's horn burst into a glow as bright as a neon sign.

The Celloraptor reared up in surprise and then ran away. The Ceratops leader started grazing on mushrooms. But he stayed watchful for the raptor's possible return.

Hannah considered the Ceratops's use of his light-up horn to scare away the Celloraptor. She remembered certain deep-sea fish that used light as a lure. Then she saw this tactic in action. What looked like a nest of blue worms wiggled and wriggled. Then, suddenly, she saw a long tongue whip out from the nest and snatch up a passing dragonfly. Hannah couldn't believe what she was seeing. The glowing blue stripes she thought were worms were actually the incredible camouflage of a striped, glowing frog!

Hannah's stomach growled. If a frog could catch food using light, maybe she could, too. Cautiously leaving her hiding place, Hannah scooped up a handful of glowing algae she found nearby. She smeared the slimy plant scum on the end of a piece of twine, then wiggled the twine to simulate the crawling of a bioluminescent bug.

Hannah did not have to wait long for a hungry creature to take her bait. A lizard leaped onto the twine. Even as Hannah grabbed it, a snake-like animal approached. Hannah quickly sliced its underbelly. She soon snagged more exotic edibles, hoping to find a hungry Trevor and Sean. While puzzling over the problem of how to find her companions, Hannah heard the Ceratops leader moan loudly. The rest of the herd looked up in alarm. Then they started to stampede!

As the Ceratopses fled the lagoon, their pounding feet bounced the ground beneath Hannah. She wondered, *What could frighten such big creatures?* Hannah looked longingly at her shelter. Should she run for it? Would it protect her?

Then she saw something she thought only lived on a few isolated islands off Indonesia: a Komodo dragon! Hannah recognized the form of the world's largest living lizard, but this underground specimen lacked all color, and seemed much longer than the Komodo's

maximum size of nine feet.

Angry at the herd's escape, the dragon stepped closer to Hannah's shelter. With one swipe of its muscular tail, the Komodo smashed it to bits!

Hannah swallowed hard. Thank goodness she wasn't inside. Then she realized the dragon's eyes stared straight at her—and the beast seemed ready to charge! Hannah knew that surface Komodos could not move that quickly. But its bite was so full of germs that even a small wound could be deadly. She had to keep the creature away from her!

Hannah threw a glow stick. Just like the Ceratops's horn, the sudden brightness dazzled the dragon. The Komodo backed away, blinded, and knocked itself out on some jagged rocks. The rocks crashed loudly with the force of the creature's enormous body.

In a nearby tunnel, Trevor and Sean, who had fallen down a deep chasm of their own to the center of the Earth, heard the crash.

"What was that?" Trevor asked.

Sean shook his head. "Nothing I want to meet."

Also curious about the crash, the Ceratops herd returned to the lagoon. Intrigued by the parade of living lanterns, Trevor and Sean followed the glowing horns to Hannah.

"You fell, too?" the guide asked.

"And how!" Sean replied. But there was no time to catch up on their separate adventures.

Trevor exclaimed, "We have to get out of here now! If Max was right, the fourth blip means that magma is building up under this region and . . ."

Sean interrupted, wiping sweat-soaked hair off his face. "Yeah, whatever. What's your plan?"

Trevor didn't have one, until he saw the yellow claws of one of the giant burrowing scorpions. "That overgrown lobster just might be our ticket out of here."

Hannah shuddered. "You want us to voluntarily go near that thing?"

Trevor shrugged. "He's a tunnel-making machine who wants

to live as much as we do. Maybe he can dig a path away from the magma."

The scorpion crashed through a wall, merging another tunnel with the one in which the travelers stood.

Hannah wiped sweat off her neck. "I'm too hot to think of anything better." So the three travelers started following the big red creature. The scorpion gave no indication of even noticing the puny humans.

The horrible heat grew worse and then seemed to break, like a fever. They kept walking, living on mushrooms and small creatures that Hannah cooked on her stove while the scorpion slept.

According to Trevor's watch, they had been in the Earth for a week when he spotted a squirrel. Trevor, Hannah, and Sean followed it to a vent that soon led them aboveground.

Trevor looked around. "I know that mountain." He'd seen the same snowy peak on the cover of countless Japanese restaurant menus. Sean thought it looked familiar, too.

Hannah gasped. "How did we get to Mount Fuji?!"

Trevor did not know. "Subterranean tunnels, volcanic vents . . . But when you consider the distances involved, we couldn't have gone that far. Unless the g-forces are different inside the Earth, accelerating the speed of our fall . . ."

"G-forces?" Sean asked.

"Speed of gravity," Trevor explained.

Hannah interrupted. "Why don't we get to safety before we talk any more science?"

"And get something real to eat," Sean suggested.

The three "volcano travelers" briefly captured the Japanese public's imagination. Then the story spread worldwide. Trevor thought this would awaken the scientific community to the truth of Verne and Max's theories. But to most people, especially other scientists, the tale seemed too fantastic to be true.

Despite a lack of funding or credibility, Trevor and Hannah devoted the rest of their lives to trying to prove the existence of the creatures they had seen in the center of the Earth. Trevor found that having just one other person believe him was enough to keep his work alive. Someday, he felt sure, the truth would be more widely known.

Sean's unbelievable adventure inspired him to become a video-game designer when he grew up. Fans loved his games because they always featured seemingly unreal monsters. Gamers especially loved the giant burrowing scorpions, giant Komodo dragons, and clear-skinned raptors.

END.

RESCUE

Hannah searched her surroundings for some way to signal Trevor and Sean and to map her path through the tunnels. She discovered that the plentiful bioluminescent algae could be used as paint. Hannah made a crude paintbrush and filled a shell with crushed, glowing algae. Then she painted arrows on the ground to mark her progress.

Hannah turned a coil of petrified bark into a megaphone. As she shouted Trevor and Sean's names, the bark magnified the sound. Unfortunately, the loud calls also attracted the attention of local predators.

The scrabble of quick claws on rocks alerted Hannah to the creatures arranging themselves in a rough circle around her. Hannah saw a raptor-like head with the fierce jaws and claws of a serious hunter. But glowing green bones shone through the transparent skin. Fascinated, repulsed, and frightened, Hannah stared at the eerie reptiles, realizing she could even see their internal organs, glowing bright colors under the green bones.

A purple tongue snaked out between spiky fangs. Hannah shuddered. These Celloraptors moved fast on legs almost as long as her whole body. Hannah knew she could not fight or outrun such beasts. But could she survive by distracting the Celloraptors?

If you think she should dazzle the Celloraptors with a glow stick and then run for it, keep reading on page 107, Chapter: Glow Stick.

If you think Hannah should shock the beasts with an amplified scream and then run for it, keep reading on page 110, Chapter: Scream.

GLOW STICK

Hannah's glow stick dazzled the Celloraptors, but they soon recovered and moved in for the attack. Hannah fumbled for another stick. How long would she be able to keep the creatures away?

Suddenly, the tunnel shook with the approach of an even larger predator, the humongous burrowing scorpion! Its yellow claws tore open the tunnel behind the lead Celloraptor.

The green-bellied scorpion had to be as big as a T. rex! One of its huge claws grabbed the nearest Celloraptor and lifted the frantically kicking creature to its mouth. The raptor roared with pain as the scorpion clamped it between six-foot fangs.

Tearing her eyes away from the grisly battle, Hannah bolted down the new tunnel just dug by the scorpion. Watching the carnage as she ran, Hannah ran into something that screamed at the same time she did. "Ahhh!"

Hannah recognized Trevor's scream just as he recognized hers. Sean asked, "How did you get here?"

Like Hannah, both Trevor and Sean had taken the "big fall" into the center of the Earth. Beyond luck lay a certain logic. Just as all rivers on the surface of the Earth lead to the oceans, the underground world was riddled with many shafts and tunnels that all met at the center of the Earth.

Hannah told Trevor, "Okay, you win." Hard as it was to admit, the guide added, "Verne was right. This place is crawling with wildlife!"

Having also seen some of the amazing beasts, Sean and Trevor were just as eager as Hannah to escape. "We have to do this logically," the guide began, "or we'll be wandering for the rest of our lives. We need to mark where we've been."

"We found a pond full of glowing algae," Trevor said. "We could smear it like fluorescent paint."

Hannah asked, "Could you find the pond again?"

Trevor sighed. "I could find it a lot easier if we'd thought of using the algae as paint sooner."

Before long, Trevor and Sean retraced their steps to the pond. Hannah fished a plastic bag out of her pack. They filled it with glowing algae and finger-painted their progress through the dark maze.

The travelers met their own marks several times and even had to follow the trail back to the pond once to replenish their paint supply. But eventually they found a long, gradually sloping path that led them slowly toward the surface.

After two grueling weeks, Sean grew tired of constantly walking uphill. "We've been walking forever," he said. "How can we be sure we're getting closer to the surface? What if we run out of paint again before we find more glowing algae? I'm *not* walking all the way back to that pond."

Hannah tilted the plastic bag to see how much algae they had left. She dipped her fingers in the slimy stuff before reassuring Sean. "We still have a good half-a-bag of paint. If we run out, we'll find some other way to blaze our trail."

Then she marked the rock wall with another glowing arrow. Suddenly, a sharp whistle sounded. A man in a National Park Service uniform stepped out of the shadows and said, "I saw that, Miss! Didn't you hear the part about not defacing these natural wonders?"

Hannah blinked, then hid her glowing fingers guiltily.

Trevor stared at the man's uniform and the patch on his shoulder. "Is this Carlsbad Caverns?" he said in disbelief. "In New Mexico?"

The guide sighed. "Well, it isn't the Empire State Building." Then he looked more closely at the three ragged travelers. "You didn't pay for the tour," he accused as a tour group caught up to him.

The truth finally sank in. Trevor smiled and hugged the astonished tour guide. "No, but it was an accident. We'd be happy to pay you now and join your group—as long as you're headed back to civilization."

The guide gave Trevor a strange look. "You can settle up at the front office when we get back to the Visitor's Center."

Sean looked at the tourists staring at the travelers. "Can anyone

spare a snack?"

The hungry teenager soon found himself heaped with candy bars and trail mix. As he greedily consumed the delicious morsels, the guide once again stared at the newest members of his group. "How did you all get here?" he asked. "You know you're not authorized to wander these caverns without a qualified guide."

Sean didn't stop eating, but answered anyway. "Would you believe we fell through the center of the Earth?"

When the travelers got to the Visitor's Center, Sean called his mother to let her know they were safe. As it turned out, she would be the only person to believe their wild adventure. She knew her son would not lie about something so serious. At first, she felt furious at Trevor for risking Sean's life. But the fact that the boy survived and even thrived soothed Elizabeth's anger.

Sean emerged from the Earth eager to explore more of the fascinating world. Instead of dreading the move to Canada, he now saw it as a chance to explore a new place.

Hannah had the opposite reaction. She wanted no more adventures. Hannah quit her job as a guide to become a librarian. Since her face-to-face with the raptors and the giant scorpion, Hannah decided she'd rather read about adventures than have any more.

Trevor returned to his university job just long enough to give his notice to Dean Kitzens. Trevor found work as a field geologist, which gave him daily contact with the Earth. Trevor made several important finds, including one fossil pointing to the existence of an until-now undiscovered species resembling a giant scorpion. Trevor, of course, maintained that he had actually seen a living specimen of the monster. Though some of his colleagues laughed at him, Trevor knew the truth.

And so did Sean. Their experience in Mount Snaeffels—and Carlsbad Caverns—brought the two much closer. Every year after that, they took a trip together. But none could match their first amazing adventure into the center of the Earth.

END.

SCREAM

As she had hoped, Hannah's megaphone scream startled the lead Celloraptor. But it also disturbed the tunnel walls. To Hannah's amazement, lumpy rocks rolled out of the walls, uncurling to become giant, gray gorillas with rocky plates covering most of their furry bodies. The apes hooted excitedly, driving off the remaining raptors.

At first, Hannah felt terrified. But the giant apes did not seem at all hostile, just curious about Hannah, her clothes, and her pack. The Rockillas sniffed her up and down. Then the leader grunted and pointed. Hannah understood. He had smelled her kind before!

The Rockillas followed their noses to Trevor and Sean. Though the beasts had seen the humans before, Trevor and Sean had been fooled by the Rockillas' clever camouflage. They had only glimpsed rocks that seemed to move.

When they saw Hannah's huge, hairy companions, Trevor and Sean gasped. Trevor worried, "Are you okay?"

Hannah nodded. "I might never have found you without these guys."

Sean stared at the massive Rockillas. "Are you sure they aren't dangerous?"

As if in answer to Sean's questions, the Rockilla leader made a series of gestures. He touched his fingers to his mouth and then rubbed his stomach. He pointed to his mouth again, then to the humans.

Sean asked, "Does he want to give us food—or eat us?"

Trevor replied, "I'm pretty sure he wants to give us food. Surface gorillas are vegetarians. Maybe these guys are, too."

Hannah shrugged. "Maybe."

If you think they should carefully back away, keep reading on page 112, Chapter: Easy Does It.

If you think Hannah, Trevor, and Sean should accept the Rockillas' hospitality, keep reading on page 114, Chapter: Ape.

EASY DOES IT

Hannah, Trevor, and Sean slowly backed away from the Rockillas. The apes interpreted their actions as rude and cowardly. With a few swift leaps of their long, strong legs, the leader and several other large males blocked the path of escape.

Trevor looked around and muttered, "Uh-oh."

Hannah wiped sweat off her brow. The heat was becoming unbearable. Yet the Rockillas did not seem bothered. Hannah wondered, "How can they stand it?"

Trevor shrugged, feeling his knees buckle.

"I don't feel so good," Sean said faintly. As he slumped toward the ground, the nearest Rockilla stopped Sean's fall. Then he slung the boy over his back.

Two more Rockillas lifted up Trevor and Hannah. Trevor tried to protest, "Whoa!" But the beast just started walking and Trevor went along for the ride.

Fortunately, the apes knew of a cool place safe from the imminent seismic disturbance. Though they did not understand plate tectonics, generations of Rockillas had survived the consequences of Earth's ever-shifting crust and moody, molten core. When the magma under the center's air-filled chamber reached the popping point, the Rockillas instinctively relocated to an area protected by thick rock walls.

When they reached this sanctuary, Trevor, Hannah, and Sean revived. But the Rockillas remained convinced that these small, helpless creatures needed protection, so they put the humans in a cage.

At first, the three prisoners felt terrified. But the tender treatment they received soon made it clear that the Rockillas regarded them not as prey but as pets. Trevor, Hannah, and Sean spent an entire

month living like hamsters until they finally managed to tunnel free of their cage.

Eventually they found their way to the surface of Mount Snaeffels through a vent. The climb was treacherous, and it took several days, but they made it.

Brought together by their ordeal, Trevor and Hannah eventually got married. Never forgetting his time in the cage, Sean became a prominent leader of the animal rights movement.

END.

APE

Hannah's bravery earned the respect of the Rockillas. Using sign language and charades, the Rockillas communicated with the humans, "Too HOT! We go now. Safe place. Follow."

Though the Rockillas had no idea why their territory periodically became an inferno, they obviously knew what to do to survive the build-up of heat and pressure that threatened their lives.

The travelers rejoiced that their huge friends could lead them to safety. But they found it extremely hard to keep up. This reminded Sean of his toddler days, having to take two or three steps for each one of his mother's. Trevor panted from a combination of heat and fatigue. "Uh, guys? Could we please slow down?"

The apes, of course, could not understand Trevor's words. But the gasping wheeze of his breath made the problem quite clear. The nearest Rockilla grabbed Trevor and slung him on his back. Trevor wrapped his legs around the beast's waist, and from then on, all three humans traveled piggyback-style.

When they reached an area full of vines, the Rockillas moved even faster, swinging and swooping like surface apes traveling through the trees. Sean closed his eyes during the first swing. But after that, he clamped his legs and arms tightly around his host and enjoyed the amazing ride!

The Rockillas moved with such grace and confidence that Sean's fears nearly disappeared, even when they swung over huge cliffs. The tireless apes climbed up, up, up, until they reached an underground Eden.

Trevor, Hannah, and Sean marveled at the size, number, and spectacular nature of the plants and animals thriving beneath the Earth's crust. The Rockillas plucked a vegetarian feast from the trees, bushes, and even from under a few rocks. Then they artfully arranged the food on ferns before presenting it to their guests. Trevor, Hannah, and Sean soon realized the Rockillas were not as primitive as they first appeared.

The Rockillas understood symbols, like maps. By drawing in the dirt, Hannah, Trevor, and Sean managed to make the Rockillas understand their need to find a way to the surface.

The Rockillas shunned the surface themselves, believing it to be a nightmare world full of monsters. But after a brief, refreshing rest, they escorted the travelers to the path that would take them safely back to civilization.

Almost as soon as they stepped outside Mount Snaeffels, the amazing adventure took on the quality of a dream. Sean mused, "Did we really just swing through vines with underground apes?"

Hannah shook her head. "I was there, yet I barely believe it myself."

Trevor asked, "Do you think we should tell people about the Rockillas?"

Hannah didn't know. "They won't believe us."

Sean added, "*I* don't believe us! And even if they did . . ."

Trevor frowned, thinking of the fate of Earth's surface apes. "That might be even worse. What if people ruined the Rockillas' habitat— or kidnapped them for studies in labs?"

Hannah reached out her hand. "Let's pledge to leave our rocky friends in peace."

Trevor and Sean topped Hannah's hand with their own and swore never to reveal all they saw inside the center of the Earth.

END.

SEAN'S SOLO SOJOURN

Sean's tunnel suddenly sloped steeply down. "Whoa!" he said as if the word could stop gravity. But it could not, and as Sean's feet lost their grip, he tripped into a black void screaming, "HELP!"

The empty darkness seemed to swallow Sean's cry. He fell for what seemed to be an impossibly long time, doing the kind of flying he'd only experienced before in dreams. It would have been fun if Sean could know for sure that this weightless drifting would not end with a painful splat.

As he fell, Sean's headlamp met another light from below. He tried to make out what this could be, but the light seemed general, not from a specific source.

Colors became visible: a big swatch of blue, partly ringed by a stripe of jungle green. Sean smelled plants and wondered, *How can anything green grow without the sun?*

Then the blue grew suddenly near and Sean splashed down into a big, subterranean lagoon. Sean kicked to keep his head above the cold, blue water. Beneath the rippled surface moved mysterious glowing masses. Sean saw something larger than a shark and, frightened, scrambled toward land. Sean swam faster than he thought he could. But he had never been so desperately motivated.

Breathless and scared, Sean flopped on the rocky shore. While his arms and legs rested, Sean's mind raced. *Dad and Verne were right!* he thought. *The center of the Earth contains a whole other world!*

Sean's breath gradually slowed, but the oppressive heat made him feel weak. His stomach growled. Sean looked around at the underground jungle. He couldn't be sure, but it seemed that eyes peeked at him from the deep foliage. Sean shuddered, feeling more afraid than he ever had. Sean fought the urge to dissolve completely into fear.

"Get a grip!" he told himself. "This is no game. You can't afford to quit. You have to survive!"

Something moved at incredible speed at the edge of Sean's vision. "What was that?" he asked.

What looked like a nest of blue worms wiggled again. Then suddenly a long tongue whipped out between the undershot jaws of a wide mouth. Sean blinked. The glowing blue stripes he had taken for worms turned out to be the camouflaged body of a creature resembling a large frog!

As Sean watched, the frog performed its trick again, flicking out the long, fast tongue to snag a glowing bug right out of the air. Sean wondered if he could live on glowbugs, too. Then he trapped one of the swarming insects between his hands. Frantic wings flapped against Sean's palms.

Thinking about eating bugs, he discovered, was one thing. But could he actually put the glowing insect into his mouth? Sean hesitated. What if the insect was poisonous to humans—or just tasted incredibly disgusting? Then he remembered that fishermen often use bugs as bait. Sean wondered if he should squish the bug and eat it, or tie it to a fishing line.

If you think Sean should open his mouth and close his eyes to eat the glowing bug, keep reading on page 118, Chapter: Bugs.

If you think Sean should use the bugs as bait to go fishing, keep reading on page 121, Chapter: Fishing.

BUGS

"Sorry, little fella," Sean told the bug as he brought his palms together to still its flapping wings.

Crunch! The bug's shell cracked. Sean opened his hands. Without taking time to look at it, Sean popped the whole bug into his mouth.

Sean chewed a few times, but the bug's shell turned out to be surprisingly hard. Something tickled the back of his throat, making Sean gag. He fished out the bug's cracked shell and hairy legs, completely grossed out. When the urge to toss his cookies passed, the hungry young man picked the "meat" out of the shell with his fingers. He soon discovered that the bug's soft center tasted great! Sean couldn't believe his good luck. The glowing bugs swarming around him tasted like a cross between pistachio nuts and some kind of bean.

He scooped bugs out of the air, thinking, *These are as addictive as potato chips!* A pile of glowing shells quickly grew at his feet and that gave him an idea. Didn't hikers mark trails by stacking rocks? Sean arranged the bug shells in neat formation, with three shells forming an arrow tip marking the direction of his travels. Maybe Trevor and Hannah would somehow find the trail. At least it would prevent Sean from wandering in circles.

Sean crushed another bug, then hesitated before opening his hands. Why did his hands glow? He ate the tender center and smiled, snatching another bug. "I get it! You guys aren't just tasty and easy to catch. You're giving my skin a natural glow!" Sean quickly discovered the advantages of glowing in the dark. He bumped into far fewer stalactites and stalagmites.

Sean wondered if Trevor and Hannah had also fallen all this way down—or would they be searching for him miles closer to the surface? Sean wiped sweat off his brow. It was incredibly hot down there.

Voices calling his name interrupted Sean's gloomy thoughts. Sean's heart leaped with relief. Though he might die down here,

at least he would not be alone. Amazingly, as he'd hoped, his companions had found Sean's shell trail! Sean backtracked until he met his companions.

Trevor hugged him, then asked, "You took the big fall, too?"

Marveling at his luminous skin, Hannah wondered, "Are you all right?"

Sean chuckled, "Positively glowing, thanks!"

Trevor then explained that the reason the temperature was getting so high was that hot liquid rock, known as magma, was literally gathering steam beneath the Earth's hollow center, getting ready to shoot to the surface, turning everything surrounding them into an oven. "We must get to a geyser before the water dries up!" Trevor concluded.

Trevor knew that rising magma threatened them like a ticking time bomb. When the heat rose just a bit more, all the subterranean water would evaporate. If the travelers reached a geyser in time, they could ride the steam all the way to the surface, like Verne's heroes. But if they waited too long . . .

Just then, a thundering herd of beasts stampeded toward the travelers! The heavy, maroon-skinned animals looked like triceratops, but with only one large horn that sometimes glowed bright yellow.

Sean exclaimed at the rushing herd of Ceratopses, "Wow! They're in a hurry, too."

Trevor snapped his fingers. "Let's follow them! Animals sense impending seismic shifts and often know how to survive. Maybe those beasts have a strategy for escaping the magma."

Hannah wasted no time. She grabbed the nearest Ceratops's tail.

Wow! Trevor thought as the guide swung herself up onto its back. Hannah reached down for Sean. Trevor hoisted Sean up behind Hannah. Then he grabbed a tail himself.

The big, bustling beasts barely seemed to notice their passengers. To the travelers' alarm, the herd seemed to be heading not toward the surface, but farther down!

"Where are we going?" Hannah shouted to be heard.

Trevor did not know. They rode through an ancient maze of tunnels and emerged somewhere on the other side of the seismic disturbance.

Trevor puzzled over their good fortune. "As long as we're not directly over the magma's path to the surface, I suppose it's possible to survive such an event."

Hannah patted the rough, wrinkly, maroon hide of her mount. "We're still here, Professor."

By following the animals, Trevor, Hannah, and Sean survived the excruciating heat underground. They lived on glowing fish and bugs until they finally found a vent to the surface.

Although the intense adventure seemed much longer, the travelers had only been underground for ten days. They emerged in a scrubby desert. A kangaroo bounced by, at which point they recognized this place as the Australian Outback!

The travelers followed a fence to a remote sheep ranch. The Australian farmer stared at their glowing skin. He asked, "Are you aliens?"

Sean shook his head. "Americans."

"And an Icelander," Hannah added.

The rancher did not completely believe their story. But he accepted Trevor's American money in exchange for a meal of fresh mutton and a long-distance phone call to Elizabeth.

The three travelers became briefly famous for their glowing, bioluminescent skin. But that faded, along with their glow, once they went back to a normal diet.

Trevor and Hannah returned to Mount Snaeffels July after July to see the shadow fall on that special spot on the first, or the kalends, of the month. But they never found the entrance to the underground world again. Perhaps the seismic disturbance closed the path for good.

After Sean graduated from college, he and Trevor teamed up to research bioluminescence. Eventually the Andersons won a Nobel Prize for developing a harmless, edible x-ray technique. Sean wished he had some way to thank the tasty insects that had not only saved his life, but inspired his and Trevor's research.

END.

FISHING

Sean made a fishing rod and line from a petrified stick and some reeds. As Sean baited and waited, a glowing-blue bird hovered nearby, tilting its head and chirping.

"Is this your spot?" Sean asked the glowbird. The bird chirped sharply and something tugged Sean's line. Sean pulled a flopping fish from the water and tossed it on the rocky bank. "Thanks, Skipper!" he told the bird, whose glow seemed to brighten. Without the bird's chirp, Sean might not have noticed the tug until too late.

Sean cut off the fish's head, then tore a tiny piece of flesh for the bird. The bird gobbled greedily, then chirped for more. By doling out tiny bits of fish, Sean gained a light source—and a friend!

The glowbird flew off quickly, then doubled back for Sean. Then it flew off in the same direction again. Sean guessed, "Do you want me to follow you?"

The bird chirped, then flew off the same way again, only this time with Sean racing after him, shouting, "Hey, wait for me!"

The bird refused to slow down, so Sean just kept running. Every now and then, the bird would fly too far ahead. Sean would fear it gone forever until its pretty glow returned. When it had been gone for several scary moments, Sean cried, "Slow down!"

Instead of the blue bird's cheerful chirp, Sean heard his uncle's voice. "Who're you talking to?"

Hannah looked concerned. "Sean!" she cried.

It turned out that Trevor and Hannah had found each other back in the mine cavern, only to fall together to the center of the Earth.

Sean's true-blue friend fluttered into view. Sean gave the bird another piece of fish and said, "His name is Skipper."

Trevor explained that the reason it was getting so hot beneath the Earth was that magma beneath the Earth's hollow center had reached a critical stage. Soon the heat and pressure would reach explosive levels, like a tea kettle left on the stove too long, whistling madly before pushing off its top entirely.

With Sean's glowing friend to light the way, the three travelers rappelled back up the chasm to cooler ground. As difficult as it was, this seemed to be the surest way to return to civilization.

Skipper helped the climbers find food along the way. The bird flew ahead, exploring side tunnels, then returning to lead the way if it found a food source. For two long months, they climbed slowly back up to the surface, surviving on fish that Sean caught.

When they neared the outside world, Sean wondered if he would have to say good-bye to his feathered friend. But the bird didn't want to part company any more than Sean did. Sean shrugged. "Mom said I could have a pet in Canada once we get settled."

Trevor laughed. "Just don't tell people where he came from—or they'll think you're a Vernian."

Sean's mother felt so glad to finally have her son back, she did not quibble about his glowing pet. Caring for the bird gave Sean's life new focus. In his adult life, he became an expert on birds and bioluminescence, creating many useful and lucrative inventions.

Sean put the profits into a state-of-the-art Trevor Anderson Lab for the Study of Plate Tectonics. The lab developed technology allowing for the early detection of seismic disruptions, which in time saved countless lives.

Grateful to be on the surface in one piece, Hannah felt humbled by the discovery that Verne and her father might have been right about the center of the Earth. She spent the rest of her life exploring Verne's works for other kernels of scientific truth. Among other things, the visionary Victorian was one of the first to suggest the possibility of serious submarine exploration.

Many in the scientific community thought Hannah was as wacky as her father. But a few felt inspired to find The Lost City of Atlantis. When they uncovered the beautiful undersea forum, scientists nick-named it "Hannah's Haven."

END.

JUMP

Hannah pumped with all her might as their three-car train hurtled toward the terrifying nothingness between the track they rode and the rest of the rails.

Sean tried not to look down at the cavern below, which offered a full selection of sharp objects upon which to fall. Trevor's pulse raced with mortal fear, the kind usually reserved for his nightmares.

Hannah kept pumping, even as the car sailed off the track. She pumped, and in a quiet, wordless way, she prayed. For a moment, the triple-train floated in the air and everything seemed to slow down. Then, with a jolt that nearly knocked them out, the wheels touched down on the far side.

Awed by their miraculous good fortune, Trevor turned around to see the woman who had made it possible. He gasped, "That was incredible, thank you . . ."

Hannah's eyes did not meet Trevor's. He broke off in mid-word at the look of alarm on her pretty face. Trevor turned and saw the track split into a three-way fork. As he wondered how to steer the thing, the train shook over a bump. Trevor heard a loud click and Sean's car split off on its own!

Another click and shake sent Trevor's car down a different track. Trevor pulled a handle he hoped was the brake. The back door of his car dropped open and he sped even faster, with the door banging behind him.

Trevor grabbed the back door, then noticed a short rod. He pulled it and the car's forward speed converted into a dizzy spin. "Whoaaaa!" shouted the passenger on the out-of-control tilt-a-whirl.

Fortunately the three tracks ran parallel to one another. Trevor glimpsed Hannah's car rolling smoothly by. Then he saw his nephew grinning like a kid riding the best roller coaster ever. At least Sean couldn't say their "vacation" was all bad! Trevor finally figured out how to get his twirling car to stop spinning, but his head would take several minutes to do the same. Hannah looked back and shouted, "Are you okay?"

Trevor's dizzy lips did not want to talk yet. So he pointed both thumbs up and managed a wobbly grin. Then he saw something that snatched away his smile. Hannah's track headed straight for a sheer cliff! He instantly recovered the power of speech. "Hannah, your track ends! Quick! Jump in!"

Hannah saw her choice: Deadly fall or dangerous jump? She bravely leaped out of her car into Trevor's with a perfectly timed jump that would have made any Hollywood stuntwoman proud. As her boots landed on the rusty floor, Trevor remarked, "You're something else."

Hannah smiled only briefly before she shouted, "Trevor! This track ends, too!"

As the car careened toward a solid rock wall, Hannah grabbed the anchor off her pack and threw it hard and fast. She tied a rope around her waist and Trevor's. "What are you doing?" Trevor asked.

Hannah tightened the rope and replied, "Showing you the proper way to save somebody's life."

The rock wall grew closer. Trevor still did not understand Hannah's plan. Then the anchor caught and the rope suddenly jerked taut. "Ahhhh!" he cried as the rope pulled him from the speeding car. Trevor and Hannah landed hard on the ground. The mining car crashed into the wall and rocks rained down on them. Trevor asked, "Are you okay?"

"I'm fine," Hannah said. "That's two you owe me."

Trevor replied, "Who's keeping track?"

"I am," Hannah answered coolly.

Trevor wondered if the life-saving counted as a separate fee. Then Sean pulled his car to an easy stop in front of his companions. "That. Was. AWESOME!" he gushed.

Beyond the broken mining car, the wall that had once been solid rock now revealed the opening to a cave glittering with gems. Sean

gasped. "What is that?" Then, without waiting for an answer, he stepped toward the treasure and a possible way out.

Sean adjusted his headlamp to get a better look at the red crystals shining as bright as the Christmas lights of a busy town. He exclaimed, "Guys! Check it out! Rubies!"

Hannah's headlamp fell across a different wall, glittering with green gems. "Emeralds!"

Sean's lamp then fell on a tunnel leading out of the jeweled cave. "Look! There's more!"

This next chamber glittered from top to bottom and on every surface in between. Even the floor seemed to be made of shining glass. Everywhere Hannah's headlamp lit up sprang to sparkling life, as if the beam awakened fairies to dance. Diamond-studded stalactites hung from the ceiling like fantastic icicles, each worth a fortune. The stones ranged in size from tiny twinkles to a rich man's engagement ring to impossibly huge, all catching beams of light like a million disco balls.

Trevor tried to make sense out of this amazing phenomenon. "Must be some kind of volcanic tubes. High temperatures in volcanic tubes enable the formation of crystals . . ."

Sean picked up two diamonds off the floor, each about the size of a pencil eraser. He held them up to the pretty Icelander. "Hey, these would make a nice pair of earrings for you, Hannah."

The practical guide sighed. "Thank you, Sean. But all this is worth nothing if we can't find our way out of here."

Sean gathered more gems, reasoning, "Still, when we get out, I'm getting a Maserati."

Meanwhile, the scientist searched for an opening in the ceiling. "These diamonds must have been pushed up by magma; that's how they rise to the surface. We must be close to the center of the crater . . ."

Hannah tilted her head back to search the ceiling, too. "Could the crater be our escape?"

Trevor said, "What we'd be looking for is some kind of vent up above."

Sean only half-listened to his uncle. He had spotted a diamond the size of a baseball! His fingers tingled with the sense of destiny. This was the kind of stone that gains a nickname, and maybe even a biographer or two. This unbelievably priceless rock seemed ripe for the plucking. It wasn't loose on the floor, but it could easily be pried out of the ground.

If you think he should resist the temptation to fill his backpack with treasure and focus on finding a vent, go to page 127, Chapter: Vent.

If you think Sean should grab the big jewel, go to page 129, Chapter: Diamond.

VENT

The same sense of destiny that made Sean aware of the diamond's power also made him hesitate. Even as his itchy fingers reached toward the gigantic jewel, Sean heard that little voice inside his head whisper, *Better not.* The whole situation reminded him of the kind of fairytale in which the hero foolishly disturbs the sleeping dragon by stealing something from his treasure. Besides, as Hannah so wisely pointed out, "All this is worth nothing if we can't find our way out of here."

Sean thought of his mother and his friends back home. What good is a Maserati without passengers? Sean looked away from the huge diamond and turned his full attention to the task of finding a vent. He asked, "What exactly does a vent look like?"

As Trevor wondered which words would not sound too technical, Sean shone his lamp on a shadow between folds of rock. Trevor's eyes tracked the beam. He burst out laughing. "It looks like that!"

On the way back up, the travelers lost all of their belongings. For Sean the worst parts were the narrow squeezes—not knowing if they would ever emerge. In these tight spots, Sean found an inner strength he did not know he had. Although he did not find his father or the center of the Earth, Sean discovered the excitement of the quest. Before, Sean resented his father's absence. Now he knew why a scientist would risk everything for the truth.

Sean had caught plate tectonics fever. When he grew up, he studied every scrap of available information, then graduated to finding his own, chasing "blips" all over the world. Sean finally proved that his father—and Jules Verne—were right about many things.

In his later years, Sean became a professor like his uncle. When he told students about his underground adventure, they often asked,

"Don't you regret not taking the jewels?"

Sean always laughed and said, "Shiny rocks are not the greatest treasure."

END.

If you wonder what happens if Sean grabs the big diamond, keep reading on page 129, Chapter: Diamond.

DIAMOND

A loud crack interrupted Trevor's lecture. Trevor turned to see Sean pull a thirty-karat diamond from the ground. Sean stuffed the stone guiltily into his pack. Then all three held their breath as a series of small crunching noises followed the first loud crack, and a web of tiny cracks spread through the crystal floor beneath their feet. "Stop moving," Trevor cautioned.

Hannah froze in an awkward crouch. "What is it?" she asked.

"Muscovite," Trevor answered.

The name meant nothing to Sean, but Hannah knew the term—and the danger it posed. So she whispered, "Muscovite is a very thin type of rock formation."

Fear made Sean impatient. "How thin?"

Trevor whispered, "So thin the slightest change in weight or pressure can shatter it. In fact, it got its name from the Russians, who used it for, um, glass."

Once again, Sean felt way too scared to be polite. So he interrupted his uncle. "I'm sure your students find that kind of stuff fascinating. I'm more worried about standing on glass."

Trevor thought of the gum chewer and said, "Actually, they don't find it that fascinating. They seem bored." Trevor's voice trailed off as the three waited tensely.

Finally, Hannah whispered, "It stopped."

Slowly, the three travelers made their way back toward solid ground. A few feet from safety, Sean shifted his pack. The diamond, too hastily stuffed inside to be secure, slid out. The jewel drifted toward the fragile floor in what seemed like slow motion.

"Nooo!" Sean cried. His hands scrambled for it, but the jewel hit the floor with a small clink.

The travelers froze and held their breath again. Tense seconds ticked by before the three exhaled gratefully. Trevor sighed. "Must be thicker than I thought."

Then, with another loud crack, the muscovite shattered completely, and the floor fell out from beneath their feet! Trevor, Hannah, and Sean dropped into the darkness, screaming, "Ahhhhhhh!"

When their lungs emptied, their screams faded to silence.

Trevor felt the air rushing past him. To his horror, he observed, "We're still falling!"

As if their panicky hearts had joined a well-conducted chorus, the three travelers all started screaming again in unison and even louder, "AHHHHHHH!"

Trevor, Hannah, and Sean tried to aim their headlamps to get an idea of their situation. Dark walls rushed past. Muscovite chips and gems drifted down beside them, but they saw no hint of their ultimate destination. Sean reached for his uncle and Hannah's hands. "Will someone tell me why we're not, like, splatting on the bottom?"

Hannah offered one logical explanation. "Our minds are stretching out the final, fleeting moments of our lives. This is all happening in the blink of an eye."

Trevor offered another theory. "Or we're just falling really, really, really far."

When the travelers aimed their lamps down, empty darkness devoured the bright beams completely. They held onto one another, bewildered, afraid, but somehow still alive.

Sean finally dared to ask, "What's at the bottom?"

Trevor replied, "Well, if Jules Verne was right, some of these tunnels go hundreds, maybe thousands of miles."

Hannah could not believe the annoying science fiction writer was intruding on her last moments of life. "But Verne was not right."

Sean needed to know. "Trevor, finish! What's at the bottom?"

"The most likely theory is it probably just—," he swallowed hard before continuing, "—ends."

Fear held Sean completely now. "Ends?!" he shrieked. "Got any other theories?"

Trevor tried to offer some comfort to his nephew. "Well, the, um,

sides of this tunnel could gently slope, eroded by water, which could still run through it, and provide a gradual breaking of our fall, sort of like a water slide."

Sean grinned, more hysterically than happily. "Water slide?" he asked, clinging wildly to any hope. "Okay. Now that's a theory!"

The guide wondered, "But Trevor, what if the water formed stalagmites that are pointing straight up at us? We'd be skewered at one-hundred-and-eighty miles per hour."

Thank you for your positive input, Trevor thought sarcastically. But he kept his mouth shut.

Sean went back to screaming. No one thought of looking at a watch, so they had no idea how long they fell before something splashed on Sean's face from below. "What is that?" he asked excitedly.

Their headlamps revealed hundreds of water drops dancing upward, like bubbles rising in champagne. Though she had been silently saying a fond farewell to her life, Hannah now felt a flutter of hope.

The drops floated gracefully up, some gathering into larger clusters, others splitting apart. But the volume of water clearly increased as the travelers continued their fall.

Sean whispered a fervent prayer. "Water slide. Water slide. Water slide."

No longer silent, the shaft rang with the thunderous sound of rushing water.

"Everyone grab hold!" Trevor shouted.

As soon as their hands linked, a funnel of water rose up to lift the travelers. Then, as if in answer to Sean's prayer, the three found themselves sliding down a chute through which flowed a lively stream.

If Sean had been at a theme park, he would have preferred a steeper, scarier slide. As it was, he felt grateful that this natural, underground water slide sloped gently down a long, horizontal shaft.

This gave the three time to wonder what they might find at its end as the glowing opening to the chute drew near. Then, *sploosh*! Their world turned completely wet and blue as the travelers shot through an underwater archway into a crystal blue lagoon.

Trevor sighed with relief when his nephew's head bobbed above the rippling blue water. But he saw no sign of the guide's blond hair in the water or on the rocky shore. Trevor told Sean, "Get to shore!"

As soon as his nephew reached the rocks, Trevor dove down. The moment his head ducked beneath the blue, Hannah's appeared above it. Then she dove and Trevor came up exclaiming, "I can't find her!"

Sean shouted, "She's right next to you!"

Hannah popped up again, this time struggling. "My pack . . . help . . . too heavy . . ."

Trevor helped her wrestle out of her soggy pack. Then they both swam to shore, falling against the black rocks, happy to be breathing and in one piece.

When he stopped panting, Trevor asked, "How many do I owe you now?"

The tired guide conceded, "You're back to one."

Sean sighed. "Ottawa's sounding pretty good right now."

After a few minutes, the travelers sat up and looked around the lagoon. Then they gazed upward in wonder. How far had they fallen? Had anyone else ever dropped such a long distance?

"Where are we?" Sean asked.

Trevor looked up and saw hundreds of tiny lights flitting around in the blackness. Hannah followed his gaze and saw the lights, too. "Those look like . . . stars? No, it must be the cave ceiling. But . . ."

Sean also puzzled over the peculiar light show. "Is it me or is the cave ceiling sort of . . . moving?"

Suddenly, the points of light moved faster, separating into a sparkling shower, then gathering again into a glowing, fluttering mass. One of the blue lights flitted just in front of Hannah's face.

Sean gasped, "They're . . . birds?" Now he recognized the pattern of their flight, like pigeons soaring up together at a sudden sound. Only these blue birds glowed! Sean marveled, "Electric birds?"

The glowing creatures darted around with great agility. As one passed near, Trevor thought he recognized a long-extinct species. "They're like tiny archaeopteryx, the most primitive bird. But they're bioluminescent, like fireflies or glowworms."

One of the glowing birds hovered just a few feet away from Sean. In shape, it looked like an ordinary finch or sparrow. But the color topped any jay or bluebird: deep blue on the head and back, and an amazing glowing neon-blue on the chest and flight feathers. Sean said, "Cool. Glowbirds."

Trevor tried to recall the era for archaeopteryx. Max would have known it off the top of his head. "These birds have been extinct for roughly 150 million years. I've only seen them before as fossils."

The bird tilted its head, then looked at Sean, who held out his hand hopefully. The glowbird near Sean flew a little closer and chirped! Sean smiled, awed with surprise and delight.

Suddenly, all the glowbirds whooshed up into a glowing mass and disappeared through an opening leading toward a light. The travelers felt drawn to it, like the proverbial moths to a flame.

When they stepped through the opening, Trevor, Hannah, and Sean could not believe their eyes. After countless hours in the cramped darkness, they suddenly found themselves in an enormous Eden: huge green ferns as tall as trees, a white waterfall high as a skyscraper, even mountains, and above it all, a glowing sky-like ceiling. Sean stammered in shock, "Where are we?"

Hannah's mind argued with her eyes. "This cannot be."

Trevor, on the other hand, had wanted to believe in this all along. He flung his arms wide and announced, "Ladies and gentlemen, I give you the center of the Earth."

Trevor went on. "Max was right, Sean! He nailed it! Your father was right!"

Sean let that shock rest briefly before he said, "Hannah, your father was right, too."

Hannah shook her head. "All these years I doubted my father's crazy ravings, but I was the fool." She ran shaking fingers through her still-damp blond hair.

Sean looked up and pointed at the bright ceiling. "What's that light?"

Trevor's mind raced with possibilities. "It's some kind of luminescent gas combination. And I'm breathing, so there must be some kind of oxygen."

Trevor's ranting reminded Sean, "This is like the bio-dome from our field trip, a terr . . ."

Trevor eagerly finished for him, "Terrarium . . . thousands of miles beneath the crust of the Earth."

Then he checked the thermometer hanging off Hannah's backpack and exclaimed, "Look at this. It's eighty-two degrees down here—this is amazing! Everything is just like Jules Verne described it."

Hannah struggled to reorder her world. "So Lidenbrock, the character from the book, was real?"

Trevor guessed, "Maybe Lidenbrock got out and told Verne."

Sean seized on this encouraging tidbit. "He got out? Now that's the best news I've heard all day."

Trevor went on. "If ecosystems like this exist, they could be anywhere on our planet. It puts into question all our assumptions about the formation of the Earth. Doesn't this just blow your mind?"

Hannah had no patience with theories. "Yes. But we, ah, still need a plan to escape, Professor."

Since their situation mirrored that in the book, Trevor took out the paperback. As they strolled a mossy path, he read aloud. At intervals, waist-high dandelions waved fluffy white heads as big as basketballs. Sean plucked one of the huge flowers and blew a trail of giant seedlings as Trevor recited, ". . . the word cavern does not convey any idea of this immense space . . . words are inadequate to describe the discoveries of him who ventures into the deep abysses of the Earth . . ."

Sean's stomach growled. "Is there anything in that book about taking a break? I'm so hungry."

Hannah pointed to a forest of thick trunks. "Let's rest up ahead at those trees. We can divide one of my protein bars and figure out what we're going to do."

Sean nodded eagerly. "Protein. Yes. Please."

As they walked closer, Trevor noticed something strange about the fifty-foot tall "trees." He tilted his head for a better look at their crowns. He saw no branches, just enormous pleated ribs. Trevor knew

that structure. "I think they're fossilized mushrooms."

"*Huge* fossilized mushrooms," Sean corrected as he ran ahead, eager to see what other monstrosities he might find. His stomach hoped for giant watermelons.

Hannah whispered to Trevor. "If it's all true . . . does that mean everything in the book is real?" Memories of vivid Vernian monsters haunted her mind. "Even the really scary parts?"

Trevor also recalled aspects of his brother's favorite book with dread. His eyes darted from one shadow to the next as he confessed, "I was thinking about those parts, too."

Just then, the ground shook slightly and Sean shouted, "Trevor! Come quick!"

Peering through the misty air, darkened by the canopy of mushroom caps overhead, Trevor soon found his nephew in a clearing. The trunk of one giant mushroom had been carved into a crude doorway.

Sean asked, "Somebody actually . . . lived here?"

Trevor stepped through the carved archway with Sean. They aimed their headlamps up a winding passageway that cut through the fossilized fungus. The passage opened on an upstairs room ringed with several other archways. Amber light filtered down through the mushroom's cap. A primitive table balanced on thin logs of petrified wood lashed with rope. Several large leaves, maps, and a journal rested on the chunk of wood forming the table's top. Among other pieces of old-fashioned camping equipment, like a canteen and a camera, they spotted a kerosene lamp that still held burnable fuel.

When Trevor lit the lamp, he saw a scene from Verne's book come to life. "This camping equipment, this place—it must have been Lidenbrock's."

On the path outside, something bright caught Hannah's eye. She walked nearer to examine an uprooted tree unlike anything else in the area. A brilliant rainbow of moss decorated its multicolored roots.

The guide stepped closer. Strange, feathery leaves had been deliberately attached to the uprooted tree. Then she saw something that made her exclaim, "Oh, no."

Meanwhile, in the mushroom shelter, Trevor found a crude canvas hammock slung between rocky arches. Who had slept here? Trevor spotted a makeshift yo-yo. His heart pounded. The hand-carved toy could mean only one thing: Max had been here! But what of his brother's fate . . .

Sean flipped through a dusty old journal filled with notes and numbers, maps and math. "I think I found Lidenbrock's notebook!" Trevor slipped the yo-yo into his pocket as Sean went on. "According to this, there's an ocean nearby. Just over that . . ."

Trevor looked at the journal and his heart sank harder and faster than at the sight of the yo-yo. "This was Lidenbrock's shelter," he told Sean. "But that handwriting isn't his." Trevor held up Max's paperback book beside the journal. Both clearly contained the same neat, energetic handwriting.

Understanding washed over Sean's face. "This is . . . my father's writing."

Just then, Hannah called Trevor's name. He saw her pale face outlined in one of the mushroom's round windows. "I need to talk to you. Outside," the guide said.

Trevor gave the journal back to Sean and walked outside. From the window, Sean watched Hannah talking to Trevor. Her sad, serious expression couldn't mean anything good. Trevor held very still, as if frozen by shock. Hannah had found Max's remains.

Trevor told Sean, who then waited for Trevor to bury Max before he followed Trevor and Hannah to the uprooted tree. Why did this hurt? He and his mom had come to accept his father's death years ago. But there had always been some kind of hope . . .

Sean turned his gaze away from the weird waters to the mound of stones. Trevor gave his nephew a rock, so he could place the last one atop his father's final resting place.

Hannah patted Sean's shoulder. "I'm so sorry, Sean."

The thirteen-year-old didn't know what to feel. "I wish I'd had a chance to know him."

Trevor wiped the sweat off his brow, then tried to express what Max meant to him. After a faltering start, he opened the journal and let Max speak for himself. "'August 14, 1997. I thought I could surprise Trevor and the rest of the world with my discovery, but I've been stuck down here for six weeks. I miss my wife, my brother, and I miss my baby boy. If I don't make it out, I will have lost out on the greatest discovery of them all. That is seeing the man my son will grow up to become.'"

Trevor concluded, "You would have loved him, Sean. And he would have been proud of you."

Then he handed the journal to his nephew. As Sean clutched the book to his pounding heart, the friendly little glowbird landed nearby.

The three travelers stood in silence for a few moments, hearing nothing but the hum of the glowing sea behind them and the flap of the glowbird's wings as it flew away.

Back in the mushroom hut, Trevor scoured the journal. Perhaps his brilliant brother could help them get back to the surface! While Sean slept in his father's hammock, Hannah and Trevor pored over Max's notes. Trevor said softly, "According to Max, the average temperate is usually low . . . in the range of seventy-five degrees."

Trevor showed her a rough diagram in the journal, showing the round globe of the Earth split open with tubes running through it. "Look at these maps Max drew. We're here, in the center of the outer core. This giant air pocket we're in is surrounded by lava. During cycles of intense seismic activity . . ."

Even as Trevor spoke those words, the ground shook with another small tremor.

Hannah asked, ". . . like the one we're in right now?"

Trevor nodded. "Magma deposits under us build up and they get very, very hot, which turns this giant air pocket into an oven."

"Is that what happened to my father?" Sean called from the hammock.

Trevor remembered being a pretty good fake sleeper as a kid. How else could you find out what grown-ups really talked about? Sean must have inherited the talent.

"I know you think I'm just a kid, but I can handle this. Really," he said.

Trevor began, "Your father was planning to escape, but he ran out of time. If Max's notes are right, and they usually are, the temperatures down here could easily hit two hundred degrees."

"We'll boil," Hannah said.

Trevor flipped to another diagram in his brother's book. This showed a cobwebbed network of vents and tubes moving up to the Earth's surface. "No, we'll follow Max's escape plan. He had mapped out a fair amount to the north of here. He must've made some kind of an expedition, maybe on a raft."

Hannah did not want to upset Trevor, but she had to speak her mind. "With all due respect, Trevor, Max didn't make it. Should we really be following his plan?"

Before the scientist could answer, Sean shouted with great conviction, "Yes! My father was right about how to get down here and he was right about getting back up."

The ground shook more violently beneath them. Fear would not help them now, so Trevor tried to sound as confident as Sean when he returned to Max's notes. "According to this map, on the other side of the ocean, directly north, Max spotted a series of small rivers. These rivers could flow toward geyser holes that could lead us all the way to the surface. So if we get on one of those rivers, we could take it to the geyser, and hitch a ride all the way topside. Tricky part is we have to get there before the water gets hot enough to evaporate. Once everything goes dry down here, there's no way out."

Sean checked one of the thermometers. "It's ninety-five degrees."

Trevor sighed. "When we got here it was eight-two. It's going up fast."

Hannah asked, "How much time do you think we have?"

Trevor performed some quick calculations in his head. "Thirty-six, maybe forty-eight hours." Without wasting another second, Trevor flipped to the page with Max's design for a kite-powered raft.

While Trevor and Sean gathered reeds to make the raft, Hannah tied them into big bundles on the seashore. When enough reeds had been bundled, Hannah turned Lidenbrock's old sheets into a giant kite. As they worked, the temperature continued to climb, soon topping one hundred degrees.

Trevor cooked a trilobite, a bug-like animal that was thought to be extinct—aboveground, that is. Forcing down the strange, crablike meat, he said sarcastically, "Yum. Tasty."

Hannah explored the lush jungle just beyond the beach, emerging with filled water bottles and a harvest of exotic fruit. Seeing the rudder complete, but no mast, she asked, "Don't we need to build a center mast?"

Trevor shook his head. "The wind is stronger up high and we don't have the time to build a huge mast. This should work better."

Sean helped Trevor tie one more lashing around the rudder. Then the scientist reached into his pocket to hand his nephew an old compass—dented, scratched, and otherwise scarred by adventure. "It was your dad's," Trevor explained.

Sean whistled softly. "Wow. Thanks, Uncle Trevor."

"I remember the Christmas your mom gave it to him. She said it was so he could always find a way home," Trevor said, adding, "maybe this will get you back to her."

Sean's throat filled with unshed tears. Then his eyes grew bright. "I do have a memory of him. He showed me how the compass worked. I'd hold it out, and he'd twirl me around, and we'd watch the needle spin."

Trevor smiled. "Now it's yours. But this is what you've gotta remember . . . Down here, the polarity is reversed. So north is south and south is north. We have to sail north across this sea."

Sean corrected him, "You mean south."

Trevor grinned. "Exactly."

With a few more bags of food loaded, the travelers prepared to launch their raft. But first their kite had to catch the wind. Sean worried when he saw it lying lifelessly on the beach.

Then finally, a strong gust rippled over the water and Trevor cried,

"Okay, now!"

They flung the kite into the air. The fabric caught the wind and the kite suddenly sprang into the sky. The line snapped taut and the raft started to move toward the sea. Trevor shouted, "Get on! Hurry!"

Seconds after they all scrambled aboard, the reed raft started sailing swiftly across the underground sea. If they had not been miles under the Earth and in danger of boiling within a few days, the three travelers might have enjoyed their sea voyage. As Sean rowed, something blue swooped, then chirped above his head. Sean saw the friendly glowbird. "He's back. Hey, little guy!"

Trevor did not turn his gaze from the swelling sea and the darkening horizon. The wind tugged the kite with growing force, cooling their sweaty bodies. Hannah also saw the ominous clouds. "The current is pulling us where we want to go. Maybe we should lower the kite?"

Trevor shook his head. "No. We're up to one hundred and fourteen degrees. We need all the speed we can get."

Hannah tightened the sheet to trim the sail, which made the raft move even faster. The love for speedy ships flowed through her veins. Trevor grinned. "That's the Icelandic spirit!"

Suddenly, a storm hit. Within minutes, rain soaked their clothes, previously wet with sweat. Hannah held bravely to the kite rigging as the wind did its worst.

Trevor shouted over the ferocious gale, "Just a little storm! No big deal!"

Hannah understood that he was trying to make a joke. "That's the American spirit!"

Not knowing what else he could do, except try to stay onboard, Sean sat under a tarp. Trevor teased, "Hey, Sean, enough adventure for you yet?"

Sean replied, "I'm good, thanks."

Then Hannah saw something glowing under the churning water. She pointed. But Trevor dismissed the glowing glob. "It's looks like bioluminescent plankton."

The shapes grew larger and brighter. Sean felt almost sure

this wasn't just a mass of tiny animals. "They look pretty big for plankton. I think they're some kind of fish." He moved closer to the raft's edge.

"Sean, back up!" Trevor said. "We're not at Sea World."

Just as he said this, a huge and hideous fish leaped out of the water inches from Sean's face. He glimpsed teeth as long and sharp as needles arranged in a gaping mouth as wide as a piranha's. Spiny fins and tail, and huge, yellow eyes completed the picture of the frightening predator.

Sean swung sideways to avoid the terrible teeth. The fish flew over the raft and splashed into the sea on the other side. Hannah yelped as another hideous fish leaped toward Trevor. He threw up his arms to protect himself from its gaping mouth. The creature's jaws snapped near enough for Trevor to see each razor edge. "Agh! Off! Get it . . . its . . ." He tossed the fish back in the water.

"In the book, these, um, fish are referred to as a species of ancient pterichthys, an extinct fish." Trevor's voice trailed off as he saw a huge swarm of the razor-toothed terrors swimming straight for them.

"What else does the book say?" Sean hoped for something helpful, like how to kill them.

"It says there are a lot of them!" Hannah added.

The sea suddenly sprang to life with dozens of leaping fish. They flew over the boat, snapping their hungry jaws all the way, as if playing some sort of grisly, reverse game of dunking for apples.

Trevor tossed an oar to his nephew. He picked up another oar to swing like a baseball bat. "Sean! Show me your swing. Batter up!"

Sean swung hard at the nearest fish. *Whack!* The beast flew far off the raft. "Line drive!"

Then he heard a familiar but surprising sound. "It's my cell phone!" Sean balanced his oar under his arm and dug the phone out of his pocket. He flipped it open and called, "Hello? Hello?"

Elizabeth's voice somehow reached her son on that underground sea. "Sean? It's Mom."

"Mom? Can you hear me?" Sean shouted over crashing waves

and splashing fish. When his mother asked, "Where are you?" Sean wondered how he could possibly answer that question. Then a fish flopped onto the deck dangerously close to Hannah's backside.

Miles across Earth and deep under its crust, Elizabeth felt something every parent dreads, the twinge of distant danger touching the life of your child.

Tense seconds of miraculous air-time ticked by as Sean wondered how to help Hannah. Sean realized he'd better say something soon, before his mom completely freaked.

If you think Sean should tell her, "Help! Get a fix on this location. Trevor and I are in trouble!" keep reading on page 143, Chapter: Ask for Help.

If you think Sean should fib that he and his uncle are on a "fishing trip," go to page 145, Chapter: Fib.

ASK FOR HELP

Sean told his mother about their situation. His phone did not last long enough for rescue workers to follow the signal. But knowing that he was in trouble lit a fire under Elizabeth. Through airport and rental-car receipts, she soon discovered Sean and Trevor's destination and rallied a rescue effort to search into the strange, Icelandic mountain.

Video of the efforts wound up on television, and the tabloids went crazy for the "Vernian Explorers" lost beneath the Earth.

Meanwhile, while still in the center of the Earth, Trevor recalled how Verne's heroes escaped by riding a geyser. True, the fictional party had never reached the Earth's center. But the principles, Trevor argued, had to hold true.

Faced with rising magma threatening their swift destruction, Hannah and Sean agreed that riding a geyser might be worth a try. But with no petrified wood raft, what would they ride? That's when Sean spotted the enormous skull.

Carrying the dinosaur head toward the soon-to-be-boiling stream had been no picnic. Panting from exertion and the excruciating heat, they managed to maneuver the massive skull into position. Trying to sound more confident than he felt, Trevor said, "We're nearly at the boiling temperature. Let's all get inside the skull and prepare for 'take off.'"

Sean swallowed hard, choking down his fear with a feeble attempt at humor. "Don't we get peanuts or anything?"

Trevor gritted his teeth as steam rose and the skull began to shake. He shouted, "Hang on!" as the steam gathered force and the skull started to rise.

Sean felt that sickening, stomach-to-the-floor rush when the ship shot into the air. The three travelers clutched the giant jaws to stay within the rising rocket.

With their future still far from certain, Trevor risked a tentative,

"Yahoo!"

Hannah gave him a skeptical look.

Trevor shrugged. "Okay. We're not out the woods yet. But at least we weren't fried instantly."

Sean glared at his uncle. "You mean you weren't sure the skull could take the heat?"

The skull kept speeding up through dark miles of the underground shaft. Sean feared it might hit a rock ceiling any minute. But the shaft continued up, up, and up until the travelers saw blue sky!

When the skull cleared the mountain, Trevor shouted again, "Hang on!" Their bone ship sailed up into the sky before crashing down on the green and bouncy branches of a grapevine.

The ship smashed into many more carefully cultivated vines as it slid down a steep mountainside. Its three passengers bounced helplessly inside, clinging to one another and their curious craft.

From the base of the hill, a man ran toward the sliding skull, shaking his fists and shouting in Italian. Trevor looked up at the mountain in amazement. This volcano wasn't Snaeffels, but Stromboli!

Paying to replace the vines and for the costly rescue effort put a serious dent in Sean's gem collection. Then the vineyard owner spread the story of the jeweled caves and touched off a frenzy even wilder than the 1890s Gold Rush. Newspapers and TV coverage mentioning gems for the plucking excited desperate and greedy people across the globe. Jules's Jewel Hunters invaded Iceland. Ignorant of climbing, archeology, and everything except "Vernian Fever," many were seriously injured. Some simply became lost in trackless wilderness or subterranean tunnels. Dozens slipped into crevasses and other treacherous features of the harsh, Icelandic landscape.

Sean, Trevor, and Hannah were unfairly blamed for the disasters, leaving Trevor's scientific career permanently destroyed. After all the negative publicity, Sean wound up changing his name just to lead a semblance of a normal life. He chose a variation on Verne's rival, calling himself not H.G., but Herb Wells.

END.

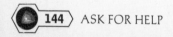

FIB

As the only child of a single parent, Sean had plenty of practice findng ways not to worry his mom. He quickly fibbed, "Trevor and I, we're on a sort of 'fishing trip' and—"

Just before it could reach Hannah, Trevor flung the hungry fish off the raft by its tail.

Sean sighed with relief. "Wow, Uncle Trevor caught a big one!"

Elizabeth still felt concerned. "Are you having fu—" Before she could finish the word "fun," another ferocious fish leaped out of the water and knocked the phone out of Sean's hand! The gadget instantly sank beneath a sea wild with glowing fish and wind-swept foam.

For a moment, Trevor feared Sean would be lost, too. So he picked up another fish and flung it at his nephew playfully. "Sean! Here's an easy one!"

Sean swung his oar and sent the fish flying. "Out of the ballpark!"

Trevor grinned, glad to see Sean back in the game. Then he saw something in the sea behind his nephew at the same time that Hannah saw it, too. They both shouted, "Sean!"

"I've got it!" Sean turned, confident that he could bat the flying fish back into the sea. But then he saw something so big, ugly, slimy, and scary that he screamed, "Ahhhh!!!! What's that?"

One of the razor-toothed fish leaped high above the raft, trying to flee the enormous sea serpent. Sean froze as the fish flew past his face. Giant jaws snapped shut and the flying fish vanished. The serpent gobbled another flying fish out of midair.

"It doesn't want us," Trevor concluded. "It wants the fish."

Trevor felt more certain of this when three more sea serpents broke the surface behind the school of glowing fish. "We have to get out of their way!" As the humongous serpents swam through the swarm of fish, the sea around the raft rose and fell even more wildly than before. Lightning flashed, as if to remind them that monsters weren't the only danger threatening their "fishing trip."

One of the serpents lunged for a fish. Its huge, slimy neck smashed into one of the masts securing the kite lines. Trevor ran to the mast and grabbed the line.

Lightning flashed again, this time striking the water.

Hannah struggled to control the kite line, despite the storm.

"Sean, grab the tiller. Steer away from the serpents," Trevor commanded.

Sean turned the tiller to point away from the pod of monsters. The raft changed course.

Trevor exclaimed, "We're pulling clear of them!"

Sean cheered, "You're the man, Uncle Trev."

"That's what I've been telling the scientific community for years!" Trevor agreed as he tied off his rope. His triumph did not last long. An even bigger gust of wind grabbed the kite and tore the line right through Hannah's hands, badly skinning them.

"Aaarrghh!" the guide screamed in pain. She fell back, clutching her injured hands.

"Hannah!" Trevor rushed to her aid, gently wrapping her hands in cloth.

Wind whipped the kite and Sean turned just in time to see Hannah's line start to pull loose. The kite's proud belly suddenly went flat as it deflated faster than any balloon. The kite dropped like a duck shot dead out of the sky.

Sean shouted, "The lines!" Then he grabbed Hannah's line and wrapped it around his wrist, pulling it taut. "I got it. Help her with her hands. I got it!"

But their raft had other problems. The damaged mast holding the other line threatened to give way completely. Sean stepped toward it, his wrist still attached to the other line. Trevor saw the danger of his nephew's situation. He shouted, "Sean . . . NO!"

But Sean could not hear the warning. He bravely reached for the second rope. Sean wrapped it around his arm and . . .

"Sean! Let it go!" Trevor shouted.

Just then the second mast broke and the kite soared high above the raft—with Sean tied to it, drifting away!

"Sean!" Trevor screamed frantically, as he dove to catch his nephew.

Sean shot up into the sky. As he hung over the wild waves, Sean struggled to undo the lines. "Help! Trevor, help meeee!"

The next thing Sean knew, he lay sprawled on his back, drenched in sweat and smelling something rotten. He opened his eyes and found himself face-to-gaping-mouth with a big, dead fish. Even though the horrible beast clearly could no longer hurt him, Sean screamed at the shock of its long, sharp teeth so close to his face.

He sat up and looked around. Sean felt glad to see his soggy backpack beside him. He followed the lines to the kite, snarled on some nearby rocks. But where was the raft and its other passengers? "Hello!" Sean shouted. "Trevor? Hannah?!"

Sean felt too thirsty to shout much more. He looked inland and spotted an opening in the craggy rocks. He tried to call again, "Trevor?" But Sean's dry mouth could barely produce more than a croak.

Sweat poured down Sean's face. He didn't need to see a thermometer to know conditions had become dangerously hot. He tried to swallow, but had no saliva left.

Seawater rippled in a shell lying on the shore. Sean knew better, but thirst tempted him to try it. He took a small sip of the salty brine, then spit it out, gagging.

Fighting panic, Sean told himself, *Okay, remember the plan. Gotta head north and find those rivers. That's where they're headed.*

Sean reached for the compass in his pocket when he glimpsed a light. He called out hopefully, "Hello?" But when he turned, all Sean saw was a glowing mass of wiggling blue stripes and two big, blue dots. Sean squinted, trying to make better sense of what he saw. The worms seemed to be all stuck together in a lumpy, black mass. Then suddenly the whole mess moved and something flicked out to snag a glowing insect in mid-flight.

Sean suddenly recognized the nest of worms as clever camouflage for a big, frog-like beast. Now that he'd seen it feed, Sean easily spotted the creature's undershot mouth, ugly as a bulldog's. And above it, the big blue dots now clearly comprised its bulging eyes.

The thirsty young man studied the glowing frog. If it resembled surface frogs, its moist skin would require this animal to have a source of water. Just as Sean wondered, *should I follow it?*, the glowfrog leaped in a dazzling display of glowing blue motion!

Sean took one step toward the frog when something bright swooped over his head. Sean looked up and smiled at the friendly glowbird. "Hey, little guy . . . where are we?"

The bird chirped, as if trying to answer Sean's question. It flew a short distance away from the shore, then chirped again. Sean didn't know which animal to follow.

If you think Sean should follow the moist-skinned glowfrog, go to page 149, Chapter: Glowfrog.

If you think Sean should follow the glowbird, keep reading on page 151, Chapter: Glowbird.

GLOWFROG

The glowfrog led Sean to drinkable water. Nothing had ever tasted better in all of Sean's life. Reluctant to leave the refreshing stream, Sean lingered long enough to notice a clutch of reptile eggs. Since many surface reptiles ignore their eggs once they are laid, Sean felt reasonably safe eating one of the eggs. Raw and slimy as it was, Sean felt its protein almost instantly revive his strength.

Sean thought, *Wow! I could take on a . . .*

He looked up and swallowed hard, because glaring at the nest was a giant, colorless Komodo dragon! Sean stared at this creature straight out of a nightmare and thought guiltily, *Oops! I guess this reptile mom doesn't ignore her eggs.*

The dragon lashed its powerful tail. Sean found himself up and running on surge of pure adrenaline. He flew through the first passage he saw.

Sean ran blindly until he realized the Komodo had not followed him. *Perhaps she doesn't want to leave her nest unattended again,* he thought.

Sean bent over to catch his ragged breath. Would he ever see to Hannah and his uncle again? Sean's throat felt so dry he could barely swallow.

The movement of glowing, blue stripes nearby caught his attention. As Sean hoped, this glowfrog also led him to water. Sean bent toward the cool stream so eagerly he banged his head on a stalactite. Sean splashed water on the bump and drank greedily. But satisfying his thirst didn't satisfy Sean. He had to find his companions! But how could anyone find anything in a dark maze?

Sean snapped his fingers, suddenly remembering an ancient Greek myth about a guy who aced this monster's maze by unwinding a thread as he walked into it. Sean sifted through his pack and found the dental floss Mom had made him pack at the last minute.

He tied a bright knot of it around the stalactite hanging over the stream. Sean walked and unwound, until he ran out of floss. His brown knit hat had plenty of yarn, so he used his knife to undo a stitch and started walking and unwinding again.

When the hat ran out, Sean tried to unravel his T-shirt. But the tight threads refused to unwind. His socks, however, proved as easy to unravel as his hat. So Sean resumed traveling. When he neared the heel of the second sock, Sean felt something tug the thread!

He froze. Would it be a Minotaur or some freaky underground monster?

"Sean?" Trevor's voice ended Sean's worries.

Together Trevor and Hannah had searched for Sean, despairing of ever finding him until Hannah spotted the thread. "That was a clever idea," she told Sean.

The teenager blushed. "I'm just glad you found me before I ran out of clothes."

Soon the three made their way back to the surface, riding an upside-down dinosaur skull through a geyser, finally coming out of the center of the Earth atop Mount Vesuvius in Italy. Amazingly, they were none the worse for their adventure. In fact, Sean found his passion. He decided to become a scientist, like his father and uncle. Only Sean would study reptiles. Though many of his colleagues called him a "Vernian madman," Sean eventually proved that giant Komodo dragons and other amazing beasts existed inside the Earth. Though a success as a scientist, Sean lost a fortune trying to promote reptile eggs as a viable alternative food source. No one ever seemed to appreciate them as much as Sean, perhaps because they had never tasted one in the center of the Earth.

END.

GLOWBIRD

"Sorry, I don't speak Jurassic," Sean told the bird. But they seemed to understand each other anyway. The glowbird flew ahead, then looked back at Sean and chirped.

"Follow you? Is that what you're saying? Do you know where I can find some water?" Sean licked his dry lips and muttered, "How desperate am I to be talking to a bird? I must be losing it."

Sean followed the bird around a rocky bend. The horrible heat made each step require tremendous effort. Sean grumbled as the bird flew so easily overhead. "Slow up, c'mon. Where're you going?" Sean asked as the bird flew around a rocky bend.

Then Sean cleared the bend, too, and saw a tiny trickle of clear water dripping down a rock into a stream. Sean looked up from the miraculous sight to the glowing bird. "Water . . . is . . . is it real?"

He dropped to his knees and cupped his hands. Sean remembered the bitter brine, so he sipped cautiously. But this sweet, cool water tasted better than anything! Sean drank his fill, then consulted his compass. He reminded himself of the reversed polarity as he watched the arrow stop moving. "South . . . good . . . The river is due north. That's where I'm going."

Fortunately, the glowbird wanted to fly in the same direction. But after hiking for only a while, Sean had the strangest feeling. It seemed as if the rocks were sinking as Sean stepped on them!

He took another step and the stone underneath him dropped enough to make Sean fall, too. Sean's pocketknife dropped out of his pocket, but instead of falling, the knife hung in the air, several inches above the rock.

Sean searched his mind for a logical explanation. "Oh, I get it. It's magnetic."

Sean took another step, feeling the rock bob and slide beneath him. Then he looked down and saw something completely terrifying. Underneath the floating rocks was . . . *nothing*!

For hundreds of feet down, Sean saw only floating rocks suspended above empty air. The glowbird chirped from the other side of the large cavern. The bird seemed eager to fly farther south. But Sean could not fly, and how could he be sure the floating bridge would hold him? Should he trust the invisible forces of magnetism, inertia, and a glowbird to find the courage to "walk on air"?

If you think Sean needs to "find another way" besides crossing the magnetic floating rocks, keep reading on page 153, Chapter: Not Rocks.

If you think Sean should follow the compass, bird, and instinct across the weird rocks, continue on page 155, Chapter: Rocks.

NOT ROCKS

The glowbird led Sean to one of its large relatives, a huge creature that seemed more like a pterodactyl than a true bird. But once inside the Earth, Sean came to accept all manner of amazing things.

The glowbird chirped and the giant seemed to understand. It perched near Sean and waited. Sean shook his head. "You can't mean that I should get on its back . . ."

The glowbird chirped more sharply. Sean stepped toward the giant flyer, then cautiously flung one leg over the big beast's back. The glowbird seemed happy—it settled on Sean's shoulder before chirping again. At this, the pterodactyl-like creature rose into the air! Sean found himself swooping higher and higher, clinging to the beast's muscular back as it flapped its giant wings.

Too scared to look down, Sean stared upward. The pterodactyl, the glowbird, and Sean had flown for several days, stopping only to rest and eat, when the glowbird spotted pools full of fish and lizards. Sean ate these as greedily as his companions.

Eventually, Sean saw a sliver of real daylight. As if this marked the edge of its territory, the big beast landed. Sean stepped off its back, almost stumbling from the shock of standing on solid ground once more. Without waiting for thanks, the big creature flapped back down into the subterranean depths.

The glowbird quickly showed Sean a path leading up to the dazzling daylight. He looked around, expecting to recognize the peak of Mount Snaeffels. But the craggy cliffs did not seem familiar.

Sean heard a distant engine and looked up to see a private plane descending. Sean followed the plane's path and after many lonely hours of walking, he found the small, lonely airport. He puzzled over the sign, then exclaimed, "Greenland!" Sean turned to the bird. "Your big blue buddy took me pretty far out of the way—not that I'm complaining," he added hastily.

Sean hoped that Trevor and Hannah had somehow escaped Mount Snaeffels as well. But, except for his glowing, blue friend, Sean seemed to be the only survivor of the ill-fated expedition.

Sean could not know how hard Trevor and Hannah searched for him, even as the molten rocks beneath the air pocket heated to critical mass. They waited much longer than good sense would dictate, until both knew that staying any longer would be suicide.

In the horrific heat, the two managed to execute Max's escape plan, riding a rushing geyser all the way up to the surface on a petrified raft. The wild ride, sped by massive molten forces and the tremendous pressure of steam in a confined space, spewed them out in the middle of the Pacific Ocean, near a tiny, deserted island.

With little more than a few coconut trees, the island nevertheless provided all they needed, and Hannah and Trevor survived for ten years. Though no formal ceremony marked their partnership, the two became closer than most married couples.

Then, one day, an off-course yacht drifted toward the island. Trevor and Hannah were rescued, along with the yacht's owners.

The three travelers shared a very special reunion in Ottawa. Sean didn't even feel embarrassed to cry with joy at the sight of his long-lost companions. Trevor and Hannah kept saying over and over, "We didn't want to leave without you. We're so glad you got out, too!"

In Trevor's absence, a grown-up Sean had continued Max's research on plate tectonics. Ironically, Trevor's disappearance helped his cause. The tragedy at Mount Snaeffels drew the attention of serious scientists. Grants followed, and Max's theories, as well as many of Verne's, were proven correct.

Trevor suddenly had his dream lab, but he just didn't feel happy. Hannah also felt out of place in society. After so many years on their private island, they found civilization sort of . . . barbaric. Trevor and Hannah married, then settled on a small island off the coast of Maine, where they spent their days much as they had on the other island: fishing, singing, and tending to a small garden.

END.

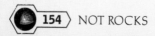

ROCKS

Sean looked across the chasm to the glowing bird, which chirped impatiently. Sean glanced at the compass again, not so much to confirm his direction as to remind himself of his father's courage. He took a tentative step onto the nearest rock.

Once again, Sean felt the weird dip under his feet. But expecting the sinking helped Sean keep his balance. He looked across the chasm at the blue bird. One sinking step at a time, Sean made his way across the void. Sometimes he had to jump to reach the next rock. Sean reminded himself to focus on his goal, and not to look down.

Near the center of the bridge, the gaps between the stones grew. Sean leaped farther, barely reaching the rock and landing on all fours. The disturbance bumped the next rock, which bumped the next.

To Sean's horror, he saw the stones slowly drifting out of range! Realizing he must act immediately, Sean took a running start and leaped desperately, swinging his arms and even reaching with his fingers for the next rock. Sean landed, but with such force the stone flipped completely over! Sean clung to its back. His headlamp dropped from his pocket and Sean watched it fall down, down, down.

The stone flipped over again, slowly turning as Sean hung on for dear life. As it twirled, Sean suddenly discovered that he had reached the other side of the canyon. He stepped gratefully back onto solid land. The glowbird chirped as if also rejoicing in Sean's safety.

At that moment, Hannah and Trevor, however, were in deep danger. Exhausted and overheated, they stopped briefly to lighten their load. "If we're going to find Sean, we have to move quickly," Trevor said, emptying out their packs. He handed Hannah their last, nearly empty water bottle. "Finish it," he said.

As Hannah savored the final drops of liquid, a giant plant rose up behind her. "DUCK!" Trevor yelled just before the Venus flytrap-like creature could strike.

Trevor grabbed a stick and thwacked the plant hard. Hannah shuddered at the close call. "Um, thanks!"

"You're welcome," Trevor said, but he couldn't resist adding, "Yeah, that'd be one more point for me."

"But who's keeping track, right?" Hannah teased as they ran away from the patch of hungry plants.

Trevor and Hannah found the river, but not Sean. Trevor said, "You should go, Hannah. Get to that river and find something, anything to use to carry you to the surface."

Hannah protested, "What? Trevor, I can't do that!"

A cloud of steam rose off the river. "The water's already evaporating. Please go!" Trevor begged. "This is all my fault. Sean is my responsibility. Now you have to get out while you still can!"

Hannah suddenly kissed Trevor. "Just in case," the guide said.

Then Trevor kissed Hannah. "Don't worry," he said. "We'll be right behind you."

Hannah muttered, "I hope so, Trevor Anderson," before she ran toward the steaming river.

Meanwhile, on the other side of the canyon, Sean followed the glowbird to a vast desert. Sean gasped as he realized that the white "rocks" all around him were giant bones!

Then the bones started shaking, and Sean turned to look for the source of such tremendous power. He expected a stampeding herd, but instead saw one giant, white dinosaur, an albino Gigantosaurus, the biggest predator ever!

The huge reptile's terrible eyes fixed on Sean. The young man looked around frantically for shelter, but saw only heaps of skeletons. Not wanting to join them, Sean ran as fast as he could toward an opening in one of the canyon's walls.

Sean crammed himself into a crevice between the rocks, hoping to hide from the living nightmare. But the big beast roared, then pushed its jaws into the shallow cave.

Sean scrambled away from the giant jaws to the back of the crevice. But the creature pushed harder, forcing its head farther into the cave. With nothing left to do, Sean screamed, "AHHHH!! HELP!"

Through the rocks, Trevor heard the faint echo of his nephew's

voice. "Sean, is that you?" Behind the cave, Trevor frantically grabbed at stones. Trevor reached through the back of the cave and pulled Sean to safety just before the Gigantosaurus crashed all the way into the cave. Together they ran for the river, but with legs the size of trucks, the Gigantosaurus ran faster.

"Hopefully Hannah is on her way out already," Trevor said.

Across the plain, Sean spotted a distant geyser of steam. He hoped the guide was riding up one like it, and that somehow he and Trevor would escape, too! But how could they do that with a Gigantosaurus on their trail?

Trevor led the beast toward a glassy plain. "It's muscovite," he told his nephew. "It can't possibly hold him."

Sean said, "Yeah, but it might not hold you, either."

"You keep running to the edge," Trevor commanded, throwing a rock to get the Gigantosaurus's attention.

Sean feared for his uncle's life. "Trevor! No!"

"Go, Sean, go!" Trevor shouted. "Get to the river!"

Sean ran, but looked back in time to see the huge dinosaur charge straight for Trevor, each step shaking the Earth. Sean cried in horror, "He's gaining on you!"

Trevor ran out farther onto the shiny surface. "Come on, crack!" he cried. Then he finally heard the first crunch of the muscovite breaking under the behemoth's massive feet. In seconds, the whole plain collapsed and the Gigantosaurus tumbled to its doom.

For one terrifying moment, Sean thought his uncle had fallen into the abyss as well. But Trevor clung to the edge!

As soon as Trevor scrambled to safer ground, a tremor shook everything. Steam choked the air and Sean saw a bubbling river. "How're we going to get to the geyser? The water is boiling."

Trevor looked around frantically. "We need a boat, or, I don't know, a log . . . anything that floats."

Just then, a figure drifted toward them through the fog. Hannah sailed a boat made from an upside-down dinosaur skull.

Sean could not believe his eyes. "She's the greatest guide on the planet!"

Hannah steered the skull closer to her companions. "You didn't

think I was going to leave without you? Get in!"

As soon as Trevor and Sean leaped into the boat, Hannah started rowing with all her might. The sweaty guide said, "I'm charging you extra for this part."

"And you're worth every last krona," Trevor agreed as the boat continued down the steaming tunnel.

Sean gasped. "How hot is it now?"

Trevor shook his head. "I don't know! The thermometer tops out at one hundred and twenty-five."

Suddenly the boat bumped. Trevor looked down and realized, "It's the bottom of the river! We're running out of water!" Then he added, "Hang on! The ride might get a bit—"

Before he could say "bumpy," the boat started falling down a steep tunnel, scraping and bumping all the way. Then it stopped, wedged between rocky walls.

Sean looked over the side of the skull and saw a bright orange glow. "What's that light down there?"

Trevor swallowed hard. "Lava . . . and it's rising."

"I thought there was supposed to be water in here, shooting up the tunnel," Sean said.

"We're too late. We missed the geyser," Trevor explained. Then the scientist wracked his brains for a solution. "Without water, there's no steam. Without steam, we're stuck. It doesn't look like there's been any water in this tunnel for hours."

"But the walls are still wet," Sean said.

"Impossible," Trevor replied. "It's one hundred and thirty degrees in here." But when Trevor touched the wall with his fingers, he found it both cold and wet.

Sean recognized his uncle's "eureka" expression.

"There's water behind that wall!" Trevor exclaimed. "Some kind of pocket. There must still be lots of it." Then he saw a familiar stripe in the damp wall. "Magnesium," he whispered.

The walls of the shaft shuddered with another tremor, nearly dislodging their skull boat. Sean looked down at the rising lava. He wished his uncle would be brilliant faster!

Trevor searched Hannah's bag and pulled out three flares. Trevor

took the first and banged it hard to ignite it. Then he threw the flare at the magnesium vein.

The flare bounced off, then fell into the lava. The second flare missed by even more. Sean felt frantic. "Maybe I should try!"

Trevor realized no lucky toss would do. He asked Hannah, "Do you have any rope left?"

Hannah always had rope, so she tied it around Trevor's feet. Then she and Sean lowered him toward the ledge. Trevor hung upside down with the final flare in his hand.

Trevor whacked the wall, but the flare wouldn't light! He turned it around, thinking that the end might be damp. He banged the other end hard. But the flare still failed to ignite.

Sean looked at the rising lava and feared that their time had run out. He gasped in the hot air, "Hurry! It's too hot to breathe!"

Trevor banged the flare over and over with all the fury of an angry ape. A red glow suddenly dazzled Trevor. "Pull me up!" he cried.

Sean and Hannah struggled to get Trevor over the skull's side without hurting him on its huge teeth. As he flopped onto the bottom of the boat, Trevor asked, "Who saved who that time?"

"Let's call it a draw," Hannah suggested.

Below the boat, the magnesium crackled and then burst into brilliant white light. With a loud *boom*, the rock wall burst open and released a flood of water just in time. When the cool water reached the hot lava, a huge plume of steam rose up in the tunnel and sent the skull ship shooting skyward!

The three travelers clung together as the ship soared upward. The skull blasted out of a volcano and flew through the air. When it landed, the skull slid down the steep slope like an out-of-control bobsled. Sean yelled, "Duck!" just as they started crashing through row after row of grapevines.

After ripping up many valuable vines, the skull finally stopped at the bottom of the mountainside.

Trevor looked back at the volcano. He recognized it as Vesuvius.

Trevor said, "If your mother asks what you did this weekend, tell her your uncle took you to Italy."

Just then, an old Italian man came up to the travelers. Even without knowing Italian, Trevor could tell the man wasn't happy about his broken grapevines.

Sean fished in his backpack and pulled out a handful of diamonds. When Trevor raised an eyebrow at the treasure, Sean said, "Geological samples. I am the son of a scientist, after all."

Sean gave the vineyard owner a big diamond.

His face beamed. Then he said in halting English, "You want to go down the other side? Go ahead, anything you want."

Sean's "geological samples" also purchased a brand-new Institute for the Study of Plate Tectonics. Trevor told Leonard to stop looking for work. "You've got a job with the Anderson and Ásgeirsson Institute for Tectonophysics Exploration!"

Trevor felt even happier when he told off Dean Kitzens. "No hard feelings about taking my lab. I really need my own building anyway," Trevor said.

"Your own building? Yeah? And how is that going to happen exactly?" Kitzens asked.

Trevor chuckled, then winked at his pretty new lab partner. "Oh, I fell into a small fortune."

When he had to say good-bye to Sean, Trevor said, "That wasn't too bad, was it, our little male bonding time? Maybe we'll do it for two weeks next time. How about Christmas break?"

Then he remembered one more thing for Sean's suitcase. "Listen, in your dad's stuff . . ." Trevor handed Sean a dog-eared paperback, margins filled with neat notes.

Sean read the title, "*The Lost City of Atlantis*?"

"Read it on the plane," Trevor suggested. "Then we'll talk."

Something wiggled inside Sean's pack. Trevor recognized the friendly bird's blue glow. It had come all the way to the surface with Sean. "Think my mom will let me keep him?" Sean asked.

END.